SPACEBY

David Walliams

SPACEBOY

Illustrated by
Adam Stower

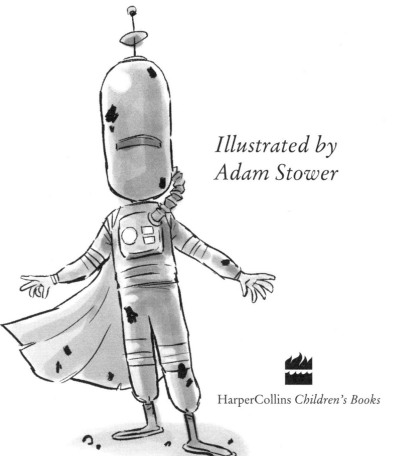

HarperCollins *Children's Books*

First published in the United Kingdom by
HarperCollins *Children's Books* in 2022
HarperCollins *Children's Books* is a division of HarperCollins*Publishers* Ltd
1 London Bridge Street
London SE1 9GF

www.harpercollins.co.uk

HarperCollins*Publishers*
1st Floor, Watermarque Building, Ringsend Road
Dublin 4, Ireland

1

HB ISBN 978-0-00-846719-7
TPB ISBN 978-0-00-857994-4
PB ISBN 978-0-00-857995-1

David Walliams and Adam Stower assert the moral right to be identified
as the author and illustrator of the work respectively.

This is a work of fiction. Names, characters, businesses, places, events, locales and
incidents are either the products of the author's imagination or used in a fictitious
manner. Apart from famous historical figures, any resemblance to actual persons,
living or dead, or actual events is purely coincidental.

A CIP catalogue record for this title is available from the British Library.

Printed and bound in the UK using 100% renewable electricity
at CPI Group (UK) Ltd

Conditions of Sale

This book is produced from independently certified FSC™ paper
to ensure responsible forest management.
For more information visit: www.harpercollins.co.uk/green

For Alfred,

My love for you is bigger than the universe.

Dad x

THANK-YOUS

I WOULD LIKE TO THANK:

CALLY POPLAK
Executive Publisher

CHARLIE REDMAYNE
CEO

ADAM STOWER
My Illustrator

PAUL STEVENS
My Literary Agent

NICK LAKE
My Editor

KATE BURNS
Art Editor

VAL BRATHWAITE
Creative Director

ELORINE GRANT
Art Director

MATTHEW KELLY
Art Director

SALLY GRIFFIN
Designer

GERALDINE STROUD
PR Director

TANYA HOUGHAM
Audio Producer

ALEX COWAN
Head of Marketing

David Walliams

IN THE 1960s the world was gripped by the space race. This was a time when the two superpowers of America and Russia battled to be first. First to launch a space rocket. First to orbit the Earth. First to send a dog into space. First to send a man into space. First to land a man on the moon. The prize was monumental: **to take control of space itself.**

Our story is set in the early years of that decade in a dusty old farm town in the Midwest of America. A place where nothing ever happens – that is, until the **ADVENTURE** of a lifetime begins...

MEET THE CHARACTERS IN THIS STORY:

RUTH

Ruth is a twelve-year-old orphan who is obsessed with outer space. She stays up all night to watch the stars from her tiny attic room in her aunt's farmhouse.

YURI

Yuri is Ruth's little three-legged dog. She found him lying in the road not far from the farmhouse. Ruth named her pet after her hero, the Russian cosmonaut Yuri Gagarin. Gagarin had just become world-famous as the very first human in space.

AUNT DOROTHY

Aunt Dorothy had lived all alone on her dusty old ostrich farm until the night her distant relative Ruth turned up on her doorstep. Reluctantly, Aunt Dorothy took the orphan in, but put her straight to work on the farm. Aunt Dorothy looks like a crocodile and snaps like one too.

THE SHERIFF

The doughnut-loving sheriff has spent his career in the police force, longing for drama. However, in this tiny town in the American Midwest, the most thrilling emergency calls he receives are for a cat stuck up a tree, a stolen bucket or a missing shoe. All that is about to change with the arrival of a creature from another world.

THE PRESIDENT

The President of the United States of America might be the most powerful person on the planet, guarded day and night by secret service agents, but he is a silly little man. He is incredibly vain with a deep tan and a ridiculous ginger toupee. All the president cares about is himself, so when an alien lands on Earth he wants to make it all about him.

ME! ME! ME!

MAJOR MAJORS

This tall, broad man has the good looks of an ageing movie star. He is the most decorated soldier in US military history and has been made the top dog at America's Top-secret Secret Base. This is where the sky is monitored for UFOs (unidentified flying objects). The Top-secret Secret Base is hidden deep underground in the desert. The place is so secret that nobody knows it even exists! That is except the president and Major Majors, of course (otherwise he wouldn't be able to find his way to work in the morning).

DR SCHOCK

Dr Schock is half man, half machine. The genius scientist worked for the Germans during the Second World War. Then he was all man, no machine, but one night he blew himself up when designing an epic rocket. Twenty years later, Dr Schock is in charge of the failing American space programme, where he barks orders at boffins.

THE BOFFINS

The boffins work at NASA (the National Aeronautics and Space Administration). These special space boffins are the boffinest boffins in the whole history of boffindom.

AND FINALLY...

SPACEBOY

A mysterious figure in a shiny silver spacesuit, boots, gloves, cape and mirrored helmet, Spaceboy speaks in a spooky voice, his face completely hidden behind his helmet.

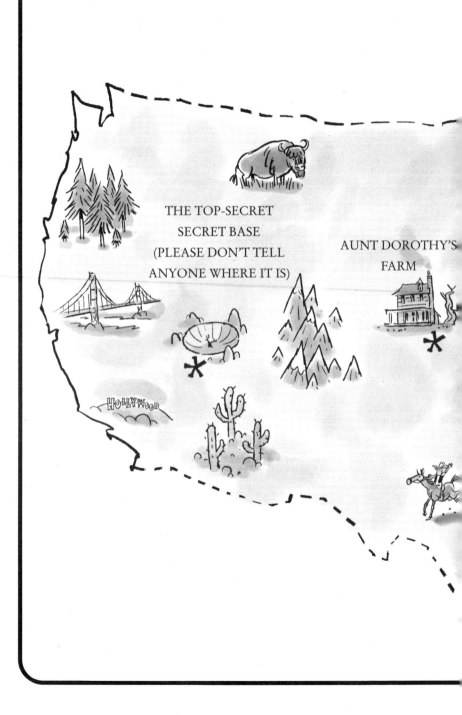

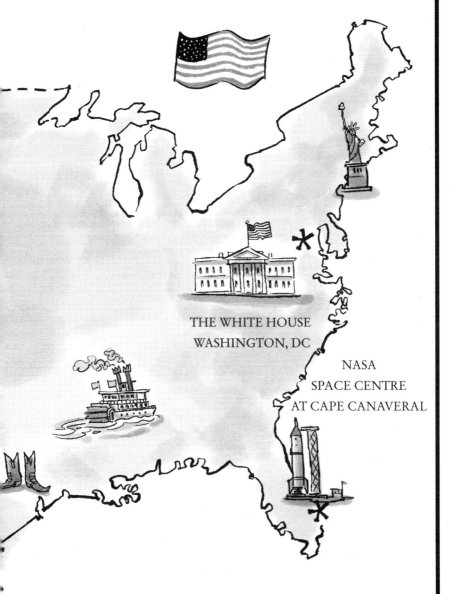

MAP OF AMERICA

THE WHITE HOUSE
WASHINGTON, DC

NASA
SPACE CENTRE
AT CAPE CANAVERAL

AUNT DOROTHY'S FARM

WHEAT FIELDS

PIGSTY

FARMHOUSE

CHICKEN COOP

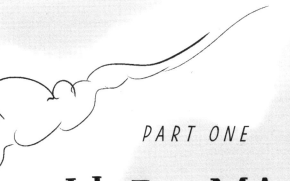

PART ONE

LIFE ON MARS

CHAPTER 1

DREAMING

A light blazed across the night sky. From her attic room at the top of the wonky farmhouse she called home, a girl named Ruth took her eye away from her telescope. She rubbed her grubby little eye with her grubby little finger.

Surely, she was dreaming.

No.

There really was something up there, spinning at terrific speed, with a streak of flames flowing from it. Whatever it was, it was **on fire!**

Could it be an aeroplane?

No, aeroplanes didn't spin like that.

Could it be a helicopter?

No, it was travelling way too fast to be a helicopter.

Could it be a shooting star?

No, it was flying too low to be a shooting star.

It was a **UFO.** An unidentified flying object!

What's more, it was coming down fast, about to crash-land **on Earth!**

This was the most thrilling moment of Ruth's little life.

The girl was an orphan. Her family were dirt poor, and her mother and father had died digging for gold. They had wanted a better life for their darling daughter, but were killed when the mine where they were working caved in. It was a grisly end. They had been buried alive.

Before that, they'd moved from state to state all their lives, looking for work. They'd slept in the back of Father's old pick-up truck. Ruth would lie there, snuggled between her mother and father for warmth. She had nothing, but she had **everything,** because she had their love. The little girl would fall asleep gazing up at the stars.

Now all Ruth had left of her beloved parents were memories. The softness of her mother's **kisses**. That special **smile** her father saved just for her.

The truck was sold to pay for the funerals, and Ruth was dispatched to her only living relative with a sign round her neck that read:

PLEASE LOOK AFTER THIS ORPHAN.

After travelling for days, most of it on foot, Ruth finally arrived one stormy night on Aunt Dorothy's doorstep. The pair had never set eyes on each other before. The old lady had never had children of her own for one very good reason.

She loathed them.

For Aunt Dorothy, all children were revolting creatures with filthy hands and snotty noses and unruly bottoms.

Aunt Dorothy's only use for the child was to put her straight to work on her **ostrich** farm. So Ruth was forced to spend her days mucking out the **ostriches** before being given the longest list of chores to complete in the farmhouse at night.

RUTH'S TO-DO LIST
BY AUNT DOROTHY

MOP THE FLOOR

SCRUB THE TOILET

PLUCK MY HAIRS OUT OF MY HAIRBRUSH

DUST THE FARMHOUSE FROM
TOP TO BOTTOM

UNBLOCK THE DRAIN

REPAIR THE ROOF

WASH MY SOCKS

SWEEP THE CHIMNEY

BRUSH AWAY THE COBWEBS

FINALLY, AS A SPECIAL TREAT,
CUT YOUR BELOVED AUNT'S TOENAILS

Ruth's life was bleak. She didn't go to school. She didn't have any friends. She didn't have a future.

All she had were her **DREAMS.**

Every night after she had finally finished her chores, Ruth would trudge all the way up the wonky staircase to her tiny attic room. She would slump down on her creaky bed, and her thoughts would turn to her mother and father. How different life would be if they were still here. Desperately, Ruth would try to keep them alive in her mind. She'd flash through all her memories of them, like turning the pages of a photograph album – not that she had a photograph of them. They were too poor for that.

Ruth's clever little three-legged dog, Yuri, could always sense when she was sad. He would take a running jump on to the bed and then nuzzle up to her.

"RUFF!"

"I love you, little Yuri," Ruth would whisper as she tickled him behind his ears. "You are all I have."

Ruth was lucky to have him, and Yuri was lucky to have her. She had found the poor thing lying in the road not far from the farmhouse. Some brute must have run the puppy over, crushing his leg under the wheel of their truck, then sped off, leaving him for dead.

On seeing him that first time, Ruth had instantly scooped the poor pup into her arms and taken him back to the farmhouse. Against all the odds, she'd nursed him back to health. The dog's left back leg couldn't be saved, so Ruth made him a new one from a battered old egg whisk and a leather belt. With that strapped in place, it was easier for him to follow Ruth around the farm while she did her chores. Not knowing if the dog had already been given a name or not, Ruth chose one for him.

Yuri.

Ruth named the dog after her hero, the handsome Russian cosmonaut **Yuri Gagarin. Gagarin** had just made headlines around the world for being the first human in space. It was the story of the century.

Dreaming

Ruth had rescued all the old newspaper and magazine front pages of his space flight in the Russian rocket **VOSTOK 1** from Aunt Dorothy's bin. Then she stuck them up all over the bare walls of her attic. There were pictures of **Gagarin** in space, pictures of him landing safely back on Earth – even a picture of him receiving a special medal, Russia's highest honour, for his incredible bravery. Handily, the pages covered all the stains, cracks and crumbled plaster, while also creating the perfect shrine to her hero. *What an ADVENTURE to be him,* she thought, *whizzing round Planet Earth while I wrestle with my aunt's toenails.* Ruth's life was as far from ADVENTURE as was imaginable.

Until tonight!

CHAPTER 2

THE DARK CURTAIN

One afternoon, while digging for bones on the farm, Yuri (the dog, not the cosmonaut) had found a battered telescope. It must have been more than a hundred years old, perhaps owned by a fallen general in the American Civil War. Yuri proudly presented it to his mistress between his teeth, his tail wagging as if he'd dug up a prize-winning bone. Painstakingly, Ruth had cleaned and repaired the telescope. After many months the girl had it working again. She could see for miles and miles and miles. The telescope became an escape, allowing her to glimpse a world far beyond her own.

At night from her tiny attic room at the top of Aunt

Dorothy's wonky farmhouse, Ruth would search the skies.

The dark curtain that hung over the Earth at night mesmerised her.

With one eye glued to the end of her telescope, Ruth spotted flashing lights, shooting stars, flying shapes, unexplained shadows and much, much more. Soon she knew the pattern of the stars in the night sky better than the features of her own face. Each night, when she couldn't keep her eyes open for a moment longer, Ruth would collapse into bed and dream the same dream. A dream in which she'd leave her cruel world behind and blast off into space in a **ROCKET SHIP.**

WHOOMPH!

Shooting high into the sky above the **ostrich** farm, Ruth would wave goodbye to her wicked Aunt Dorothy with a grin. Then she and her dog, Yuri, would zoom through the solar system.

WHIZZ!

They would sail past Mars, Jupiter, Saturn, Uranus
and Neptune. Next, they would *ZOOM* out of
the solar system and explore more of our galaxy, the
Milky Way. In the Milky Way our sun is only one of
billions of stars, some of them the centres of their

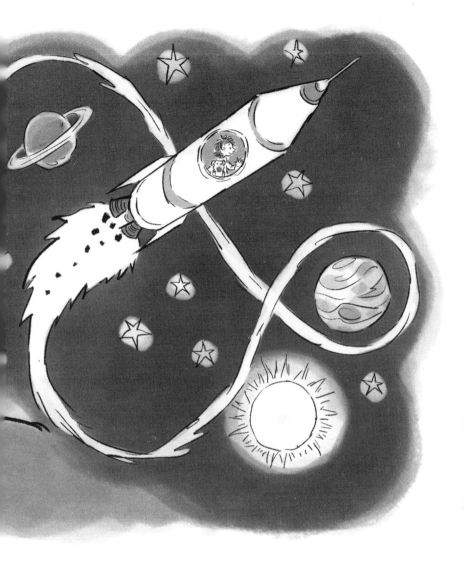

own solar systems. In turn, the Milky Way is just one of **billions** of galaxies in the universe. The universe itself is forever expanding, so there would be an infinity of space to explore.

A packed lunch was **essential.**

So now, in her room, looking at the **UFO** through her telescope, Ruth wondered if THIS was a dream. She pinched herself.

"OUCH!" she cried.

No. This was really happening. A **UFO** on fire really was hurtling through the sky. Now it was so near that Yuri could see it too. He bounded off the girl's bed, peered out of the window and began barking furiously.

"WOOF! WOOF! WOOF!"

"Shush, Yuri!" whispered Ruth. "You'll wake up Aunt Dorothy!"

It was past midnight, and the lady would be sleeping in the room directly beneath them.

"WOOF! WOOF! WOOF!"

"SHUSH! You stay there, Yuri!" she whispered. "I need to get a closer look at this thing!"

The dog shook his head wearily as Ruth clambered out of the wonky window at the front of the farmhouse. She was clutching her aunt's ancient box camera that she'd hidden under her bed for just such an occasion.

Ruth had found the camera gathering dust on a high shelf, and figured it was all right to "borrow" it. The girl was not stupid. She knew the old lady would say no, so Ruth figured it was best not to ask her at all!

SIMPLE!

Within moments, Ruth had scrambled on to the roof, clutching the camera. Like every part of the farmhouse, the roof was all wonky. She was wearing her pyjamas and no shoes. One false move and she could plunge to the ground.

What's more, it was a long way down.

Determined to get a better view of the spacecraft,

Ruth climbed to the highest point of the roof, the wonky chimney stack. She grabbed hold of it to steady herself, but DISASTER STRUCK! A chunk of stone broke off in her hand.

KERUNCH!

Ruth wobbled on her feet, toppling over.

"WHOA!"

CHAPTER 3

FLYING SAUCER ON FIRE

Desperately, Ruth waved her arms in the air, like an **ostrich** attempting take-off. She gripped on to the roof with her toes. She'd always had monkey feet. Her parents had been so poor that they'd never had enough money to buy her shoes. Over time, her feet had got good at gripping.

"PHEW!" she exclaimed.

She was still alive.

From the roof of the farmhouse, Ruth could see for miles in every direction. Vast squares of golden wheat stretched out as far as the eye could see, save for the odd clump of trees or farm buildings. With her free hand, Ruth fumbled with her aunt's ancient camera.

Now the **UFO** was zooming straight towards her.

WHIZZ!

Ruth's heart pounded in her chest.

BA-BOM! BA-BOM! BA-BOM!

This was thrilling and terrifying in equal measure. She brought the camera up to her eye and spun the lens to focus.

WHIRR!

The image sharpened into view.

Ruth gulped.

This wasn't just a **UFO.**

This was a flying saucer!

She had seen flying saucers on the covers of comic books she'd never owned and on posters for films she'd never had the pleasure of seeing. She was too poor for such luxuries of life. However, she knew one thing.

Flying saucers were NOT of this planet.

It was an **alien** spacecraft!

Inside that thing was a visitor from another world!

The flying saucer was a battered metal circle that spun at terrific speed. On top of this spinning circle was a pod, like an upside-down glass bowl. In that pod was a mysterious figure in a silver spacesuit with a tall helmet. He must have a really long head!

SCARY!

With her hands shaking in fear, Ruth just couldn't click the button to take a photograph. Now it was too late. The flying saucer on fire had hurtled over her.

WHOOSH!

The underside of the spacecraft skimmed the chimney stack.

WHOOMPH!

It sent shards of stone exploding into the air.

BANG!

One of them struck Ruth on the head…

CLONK!

…knocking her over in an instant.

THUMP!

Aunt Dorothy's antique camera slipped out of her hands.

CLANK!

It tumbled down the slope of the roof.

CLANK! CLINK! CLUNK!

Ruth scrambled to save the camera. She stretched out her hand. But it was just out of reach. The camera bounced off the edge of the roof before smashing on to the ground.

KERRASH!

"NO!" cried Ruth as she saw it explode into pieces below.

To make matters worse, she heard a roof tile break under her weight.

CRACK!

The girl lost her footing and fell...

"WHOA!"

...lurching forward.

PLOMP!

The roof was steep, and Ruth slid down it HEADFIRST on her belly.

"HELP!" she cried, even though no one could help her right now.

She went straight over the side of the roof, her arms outstretched in front of her.

As she felt herself free-falling, Ruth remembered her MONKEY FEET!

Her trusty toes just managed to cling on to the edge. "PHEW!" said Ruth, as she dangled upside down from the roof like a bat.

She swung forward, her head knocking against the glass of the attic's back window.

CLONK!

Yuri had been staring out of the front window from which Ruth had climbed out, but the noise made him turn.

Ruth couldn't open this window from the outside, and so mimed for Yuri to help.

Yuri scuttled over and, nudging with his nose, slid the window open.

S H U N T !

"Thank you, Yuri!" whispered Ruth before hauling herself into the attic. She collapsed on the floor.

THUD!

Relieved that his mistress was alive, the dog began a frenzied licking of Ruth's face.

SLURP! SLURP! SLURP!

"All right, Yuri! Good boy!" said Ruth, gently guiding Yuri's head and his rough tongue away. She scrambled to her feet and looked out of the window through which she'd just climbed. In the distance, she saw the flying saucer crash-land in the furthest field of the farm.

SLAM!

A huge cloud of dust hurled into the air.

WHOOMPH!

"Oh no!" said Ruth, aghast.

She thumped down on the bed and slipped on her boots.

"Come on, Yuri!" she said. "We need to search for survivors."

The little dog followed her over to the door.

When Ruth opened it, a shadowy figure was waiting for her on the other side.

"And where do you think you are going?" it hissed.

CHAPTER 4

THE OLD CROCODILE

"Nowhere," said Ruth, shifting uneasily in the attic doorway.

"Don't lie to me, ROOF!" the voice thundered.

Aunt Dorothy had a special way of saying the girl's name.

It was never "Ruth".

It was always "ROOF".

Or when she was being told off: "ROOOF".

Sometimes, when Aunt Dorothy was really angry, she called her "ROOOOOOOOOOF!"

"It's true. I am going nowhere!" said Ruth. Although this statement might be true in the broader sense of Ruth's life, it wasn't true right now.

"You can't be going nowhere! You must be going somewhere!" sneered Aunt Dorothy. She looked like a crocodile and snapped like one too.

Cold, dark eyes

Pale skin

Nosy nose

Grey hair

Sharp teeth
(fangs, really)

Bulging
blue veins

Wicked grin

Black
dress

Black
handbag for
whacking
folks

Black boots for booting dogs

Aunt Dorothy always dressed from head to toe in black, as if she were in mourning. Most likely for her own wretched life. There weren't any takers for **ostrich** meat in her town so Dorothy was dirt poor. She took out her own misery on everyone else.

Her long grey hair was swept back and tied in a tight, painful bun. Her skin was as white as snow and her thick blue veins bubbled up to the surface whenever she was furious.

Which was all the time.

Aunt Dorothy would proudly boast to anyone who visited her farm that she loathed children.

"Children are rude, vile creatures! Rotten maggots, the lot of 'em! That girl ROOF is the *worst*. Just the sight of her is enough to make me vomit! As soon as she is old enough, I will throw her out of my house! Forever!"

She would always say things like this in a loud voice within earshot of Ruth. The terrifying crocodile wanted the girl to hear. She lived for one simple pleasure… to make Ruth's life a misery.

On that first stormy night when the orphan had arrived on her doorstep, Aunt Dorothy had given the girl a chilling look. A chilling look of the deepest, darkest resentment. A look that had stayed in her reptilian eyes ever since.

Ruth had lived with her aunt for a few years now, but the old lady was quick to point out it was…

"MY house."

"MY food."

"MY water."

"MY fire."

"MY furniture."

Once Aunt Dorothy had even told the girl, "Stop wearing my chair out with your bottom!"

Ruth was an uninvited guest, and her aunt never let her forget it.

When Ruth had staggered back to the farmhouse one afternoon with a little three-legged dog in her arms, Aunt Dorothy had been full of rage.

"NOT ANOTHER GREEDY MOUTH TO FEED!" she yelled.

There was one condition that the old crocodile had set if Ruth was to keep the dog. The animal would have to share the girl's food. Ruth agreed in an instant, not that there was much to split from the meagre rations Aunt

Dorothy gave her. However, this served to make the bond between the girl and her dog **unbreakable.** Yuri never left Ruth's side, not least because Aunt Dorothy used to boot Yuri up the bottom whenever he was out of Ruth's sight.

BOOF!

Now, Yuri stood between Ruth's legs and growled at the old lady.

"GRRRR!"

"Shut up, doggy!" shouted Aunt Dorothy. "Or you will feel the force of my boot on your bottom!"

Yuri whimpered and scampered back into the shadows.

Then Aunt Dorothy fixed her cold, dead eyes on Ruth. "Well?" she demanded. "I can wait all night for an answer! Where are you going, ROOF?"

CHAPTER 5

A SEA OF CRUMPLED PAPER

Ruth's mind was whirring. If Aunt Dorothy didn't have a clue where she was going, then she must not have heard the flying saucer crash. The old crocodile was a little deaf, so it made sense. But how long could this be kept a secret?

"Just to fetch a cup of w-w-water, Aunt D-D-Dorothy," spluttered Ruth in reply.

The old lady scoured the tiny attic room and fixed her gaze on the bedside table.

"You have a cup of water right next to your bed. I mean MY bed!"

Ruth was not the best actress, but she pretended to be surprised. "Oh! Do I? Silly me!"

"And you've got my old boots on your feet!"

"Have I?"

"Yes!" snapped Aunt Dorothy.

"Oh! So I have! I thought my feet felt heavier than usual. Shoes can do that."

This cheek made the old crocodile sneer. "Boots mean you are up to something, Roof. You are nothing but a nasty little liar!"

Ruth smiled nervously before blushing as red as a prize tomato.

She didn't want Aunt Dorothy to find out about the **UFO.** The old lady disapproved of her obsession with outer space. If Aunt Dorothy knew a flying saucer had crash-landed on the farm, she would reach for her shotgun and before you knew it...

BLAM! BLAM! BLAM!

All this had to remain Ruth's secret.

"You've been wide awake all night, staring through that stupid telescope of yours, haven't you, Rooof?" demanded Aunt Dorothy. "You've got chores in the morning. I want you mucking out the **ostriches** at dawn! Enough is enough!"

She marched across the attic and snatched the telescope.

"Please don't!" begged Ruth, fearing the worst.

Like a strongman at the fair, Aunt Dorothy bent the telescope over her knee. Using all her might, she snapped it in two.

SNAP!

Tears bloomed in Ruth's eyes.

"WHY?" she asked.

"To teach nasty little worms like you a lesson!" snarled Aunt Dorothy. Her eyes spun around Ruth's little bedroom. Spying the pictures of **Yuri Gagarin** stuck to the walls, she stalked over to them.

"All this outer-space nonsense!" she yelled. "It's not for girls! Makes me think there is something wrong with you! It has to STOP!"

Aunt Dorothy stretched out her hand, displaying her long, sharp nails. Talons, really. She placed her hand at the top of one of the pictures before turning round and offering Ruth the wickedest grin.

"PLEASE!" pleaded Ruth.

But it was no use – the woman loved cruelty.

RIP!

Down came the first picture.

RIP!

Then the second.

RIP! RIP! RIP!

Ruth couldn't watch any more. She closed her eyes. Now it was a frenzy of destruction.

RIP! RIP! RIP!
RIP! RIP!

Yuri was a spirited soul and began barking at the old lady.

"RUFF! RUFF! RUFF!"

He bit on to the bottom of her dress.

CHOMP!

Aunt Dorothy turned round and kicked out at the dog as hard as she could.

BOOT!

Yuri leaped out of the way and Ruth scooped him up in her arms.

"DON'T YOU DARE HURT YURI!" she

shouted.

"Oh! I do dare! I do!"

RIP! RIP! RIP!

Now the floor was a sea of crumpled paper.

"If I catch you out of bed again tonight, Roooof, it will be you I rip to pieces!"

Aunt Dorothy strode out of the attic and slammed the door behind her.

BAM!

This spite made Ruth even more determined to defy her aunt.

"Come on, Yuri," she whispered as she wiped away her tears with her sleeve. "We are going to have our own SECRET ADVENTURE!"

CHAPTER 6

●

A KALEIDOSCOPE OF SHADOWS

With Yuri perched on her shoulders, Ruth shimmied down the wonky drainpipe on the side of the farmhouse. From a distance, you might have thought the girl was wearing a furry scarf.

Ruth went super slowly past Aunt Dorothy's bedroom window. The curtains were drawn. The old lady hadn't spotted the fire and smoke at the far end of the farm. Peering through the slim gap in the curtains, Ruth spied her standing dead-still in her bedroom with her ear trumpet to her ear, pointing up to the attic room. She looked like a crocodile lurking under the water, ready to snap!

Ruth carried on down the drainpipe.

On reaching the ground, she set Yuri down as gently as possible so he didn't make a sound.

CLINK! CLINK! CLINK! went Yuri as he walked along the path that led away from the farmhouse.

Silly me! Ruth thought. She'd forgotten about Yuri's egg-whisk leg! So she scooped the dog up in her arms and stepped over the bits of broken camera. When they were out of earshot, or, rather, ear-trumpet-shot of the farmhouse, Ruth set Yuri down again. Despite only having three legs and one egg whisk, the little dog kept up with Ruth's breathless pace. Together, they raced past the chicken coop, the pigsty and the **ostrich** pen. They tiptoed round the sleeping cow and bull, before crossing the golden field of wheat to the crash site. The spot was pinned by a plume of black smoke. The smoke was so thick that it blotted out many of the stars in the night sky.

Ruth's heart was beating fast. Her head was spinning. Her legs felt like jelly. Any moment now, she might be the first person on Earth to meet an **alien!**

Soon the first pieces of debris from the flying saucer came into view. Smouldering shards of metal had flattened and blackened the golden wheat. The debris from the flying saucer was spread over a wide area. It had been a **MONSTER CRASH.**

Even as more pieces revealed themselves, Ruth found it impossible to work out what went where on this **alien** spacecraft.

After a short while, Ruth reached the main point of impact. The flying saucer had hit the earth hard and fast. It had gouged out the ground and was now half buried in the soil. There were clumps of little fires burning all around it.

Ruth clambered up on to what was left of the flying saucer, which was poking out at a sharp angle. At first, her boots slipped and slid on the slope, but soon she made it up to the glass pod that squatted on top of the spacecraft.

The flickers of flames, the smoke and the dark of the night together created a kaleidoscope of shadows. It was hard to know what was real and what was not. Suddenly,

Ruth felt a stab of fear. She was relieved to feel her little dog brushing right up against her leg. Yuri always made her feel safe.

Or safer, at least.

The glass of the pod was cracked and blackened with soot from the fire. It was impossible to see if the

figure Ruth had spotted from the roof of the farmhouse just moments ago was still inside. Slowly, she reached out her hand to touch the pod.

Yuri was clearly spooked by the thought of Ruth touching the thing as she could feel her little friend tugging on her pyjama trousers to stop her. However, she was headstrong, and despite the danger she placed her hand on the glass.

"OUCH!" she exclaimed. It was blazing hot, like the handle of a saucepan on the stove. Well, the flying saucer must have just burned through the Earth's atmosphere. Ruth knew from reading about **Yuri Gagarin's** journey that re-entering the Earth's atmosphere was the most dangerous part. Although **Gagarin** ended up landing safely back on Earth, the **VOSTOK 1** had glowed red from the hellish heat.

"WOOF!" barked Yuri at Ruth, as if to say, "I told you so!"

"All right! All right! Not everyone is as smart as you!"

Next, Ruth yanked the sleeve of her pyjamas down and wiped the soot off the glass with it. Soon there was a small clear patch in the black. Ruth peered into the pod to see if there was any sign of life.

There was none.

Just as Ruth was about to turn away, a gloved hand thumped on the glass.

DOOF!

"ARGH!" she screamed.

CHAPTER 7

A BILLION QUESTIONS

The shock made Ruth topple backwards. She tripped over Yuri and tumbled off the flying saucer…

"ARGH!"

The relief of finally being on the ground immediately evaporated when Ruth discovered her bottom was on fire.

"OWEEE!"

She was lying in one of the smouldering craters left by the crash! She leaped up and began hopping from foot to foot, slapping her own bottom.

THWACK! THWACK! THWACK!

Whatever was in that pod chose this as its moment to escape. The cracked glass was smashed by a gloved fist.

SHATTER!

Out clambered the thing. Its body was surprisingly short. Up to its shoulders, it was no taller than Ruth, and she was small for her age. However, its helmet towered into the sky. It was probably half as tall again as the **alien's** body. There had to be a bizarre-looking creature under there.

Yuri clambered up on to the flying saucer and scuttled over to the mysterious figure. The little dog began jumping up and down, yapping!

"WOOF! WOOF! WOOF!"

The **alien** looked truly out of this world.

Its outfit would be perfect for the bitter cold of space – not so much a balmy summer night in the American Midwest.

Every part of the **alien's** body was covered, although there was a reflective glass slot in the helmet for it to see out. But how many eyes did this thing from outer space have?

One?

Three?

Three hundred?

Its head looked big enough for three thousand!

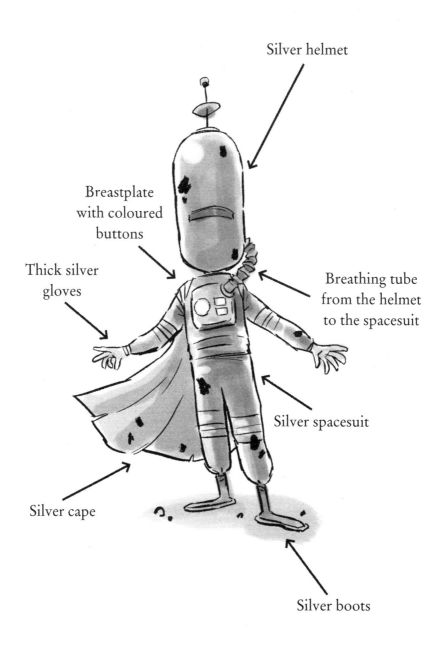

Silver helmet

Breastplate
with coloured
buttons

Thick silver
gloves

Breathing tube
from the helmet
to the spacesuit

Silver spacesuit

Silver cape

Silver boots

Ruth's brain was buzzing with a **billion** questions.
She blurted them out at a **dizzying** rate.

But before the **alien** could answer any of these, it bent down to stroke Yuri, and clutched its knee in pain.

"ARGH!"

No doubt it had been injured in the crash. The flying saucer had come down so fast and so hard that the **alien** was lucky to be alive. The thing began hobbling down from the pod, before losing its footing and tumbling to the ground.

THUD!

"Oh! I nearly forgot! Welcome to Planet Earth!" said Ruth.

Her little dog was not so welcoming and growled at this mysterious figure.

"GRRR!"

"It's all right, Yuri," said Ruth.

Now the **alien** was clutching its knee and lying in the field.

"Let me help you!" said the girl, and she reached out her hand to help the **alien** up. It looked down at her hand and hesitated for a moment. Then it began to stretch out its hand to meet hers. This would be the first handshake between a human and an **alien.** Their hands were just about to meet when…

CHAPTER 8

EXPLODED CIGAR

There was a mighty **explosion!**

What was left of the flying saucer burst into flames.

WHOOMPH!

Without thinking, Ruth wrapped her arms round the thing, leaped away from the blast and propelled them both to the ground.

DOOF!

Like a fire blanket, she covered the **alien** and her dog as a blast of flames swept over them.

Ruth closed her eyes, but could feel her hair being singed by the intense heat.

CRACKLE!

"WOOF! WOOF! WOOF!" howled Yuri in pain. The tip of his tail had been scorched.

SIZZLE!

Now his tail looked like an exploded cigar.

The little dog wriggled free of Ruth's grasp and darted off in the direction of the well. He barked all the way, running as fast as his three little legs and one egg whisk could carry him.

"YURI!" cried Ruth after him.

However, the little dog was clearly startled by having his tail set alight and was not going to stop any time soon. He disappeared off across the field and out of sight. Oh no. Ruth spotted lights flicker on in the farmhouse. Aunt Dorothy must have heard the explosion.

Ruth didn't have much time. Any moment now, her aunt would be stalking across the fields with her shotgun. She turned her attention to the **alien**.

"Are you all right?" she asked.

All it did was moan. "URGH!"

Then…

KABOOM!

There was another blast behind her.

WHOOMPH!

The heat made her feel as if her back were being flame-grilled like a burger.

It wasn't safe being this near to the flying saucer. There was every chance it could explode again. More fuel could catch fire at any moment.

Ruth scrambled to her feet and reached out her hand again to help the **alien** up. It put its hand in hers.

FIRST CONTACT!

"This is HISTORY!" chirped Ruth. "Shaking hands on Earth is a sign of friendship. Does this mean we are friends?"

The **alien** nodded its head. Ruth smiled the biggest smile.

"YES!" she exclaimed.

It was a giant YES!

Ruth had never had a friend before. An **alien** from another planet wasn't who she was expecting to be her first friend. She thought it might be a girl with a wonky fringe who collected stamps. Still, she wasn't going to argue.

"Magnificent!" she said. "And friends look out for each other. Here!"

Ruth heaved the **alien** to its feet. Immediately, its knee buckled.

"ARGH!" it cried as it toppled forward.

The girl caught it in her arms. With all her strength, she held it up.

"I've got you!" she said, but she hadn't. The **alien** couldn't stand on its knee. Instead, it slipped out of her arms

and slopped down to the ground.

THUNT!

"DARN!" she cried.

Just then she spotted a shadowy figure in the distance. It was coming from the direction of the farmhouse.

"ROOOOOOF!" came a shout.

She'd have known that voice anywhere. It was, of course, Aunt Dorothy.

BANG!

Just as Ruth had thought, the old lady had brought her shotgun! And she wasn't afraid to use it.

BANG! BANG! BANG!

She was firing warning shots into the air.

Ruth was going to have to hide her new friend.

And fast.

Like, faster than that.

Like, really fast.

FAST!

CHAPTER 9

FRAZZLED

The flying saucer had crashed a stone's throw from an old deserted hay barn. It was just one of a handful of Aunt Dorothy's farm buildings that had fallen into disrepair. And, right now, it was Ruth's best bet for a hiding place. So she pretended not to hear her aunt's shouts.

"ROOOF! ROOOOOOF! WHERE ARE YOU? I HOPE THAT PLANE CRASHED RIGHT ON TOP OF YOUR HEAD! I BROUGHT MY SHOTGUN IN CASE IT'S RUSSIANS! DON'T THINK YOU'VE GOTTEN AWAY WITH SMASHING MY CAMERA TO BITS! WAIT UNTIL I GET MY HANDS ON YOU!"

Ruth also ignored the warning shots Aunt Dorothy was still firing into the sky.

BANG! BANG! BANG!

She dragged the **alien** across the field by its feet.

"OOF! OOOF! OOF!" it moaned as its head banged on the ground.

In moments, they reached the barn. Ruth pushed open the crumbling wooden door with her back.

CREAK!

She dragged it inside, then hoisted it up from underneath its armpits before lowering it gently on to some bales of hay.

"OOF!" cried the **alien** in relief.

The roof of the barn had caved in years ago, so it was now little more than a collection of crumbling walls. However, right now, it was the best hiding place for an **alien**.

"Wait here," Ruth whispered, not that the figure looked capable of anything other than lying right there. "I'll be back."

There was a little nod of the tall helmet, followed by a moan.

"URGH!"

The **alien** raised a hand as if to implore her to stay.

"I promise!" added Ruth. She rested a hand on the

alien's shoulder for reassurance. "I have never let a friend down. Well, I've never had a friend, but if I'd ever had one, I'd never have let them down."

The **alien** tilted its head like a dog trying to understand its master.

Next, Ruth tiptoed back across to the door. She peered round it to see if the coast was clear, and then stepped out into the gloom.

A figure was standing in the shadows holding a shotgun.

It was the dreaded Aunt Dorothy.

"Who were you talking to?" demanded the old lady.

"No one!" replied Ruth, a little too rapidly to appear innocent.

"No one? You can't have been talking to no one! I might be a little deaf, but I heard voices! You are hiding someone in my barn!"

Aunt Dorothy stalked over to the door, which was dangling off its hinges. She pushed it open with the end of her shotgun.

CREAK!

Just as she stepped inside...

KABOOM!

Out in the fields, what was left of the flying saucer exploded once again.

Another fireball lit up the entire farm.

A black cloud of smoke mushroomed into the sky.

The wheat field caught fire.

WHOOMPH!

"FIRE!" shouted Aunt Dorothy as she stumbled out of the barn. "FIRE!"

"There's no fire station for miles!" replied Ruth.

"We'll have to put it out ourselves! Or my whole farm will burn to the ground! Do something, you lazy slob!"

"This way!" shouted Ruth, leading Aunt Dorothy by the wrist clear of the barn. "To the well!"

Once they arrived at the farm's well, Ruth saw her little dog was there. Yuri was nursing his singed tail in a bucket of water, a look of sweet relief on his face.

"I am sorry, Yuri!" called Ruth. "We are going to need that bucket! Quick, let's form a chain!" Soon, the girl had assigned places for everyone.

Aunt Dorothy put down her shotgun and filled the bucket from the well.

Then Yuri carried the bucket, its handle between his teeth.

Finally, Ruth hurled the water on the burning stalks of wheat.

SPLOOSH!
SIZZLE!

The empty bucket would then be given back to Yuri, and the whole process started again.

It was dawn by the time there were nothing more than large patches of smouldering black on the wheat field.

The fire was out.

All three were frazzled.

None had slept a wink.

They were all covered in soot from the fires. You would be forgiven for thinking that Yuri was a little black dog, rather than a little white dog.

The sun rose over the rolling fields, bathing everything in red light. Grimacing at the brightness, Aunt Dorothy barked at her niece.

"ROOOF! I don't want no soot in MY house! Stand still!"

Ruth did what she was told. She knew what was coming. This was what Aunt Dorothy called "bathtime", and Ruth only got one once a year. The girl closed her eyes and stretched out her arms. A moment later, a shock of cold water from the bucket drenched her.

SPLASH!

"HUH!" Ruth took a sharp breath at the chill.

When she opened her eyes, she looked down at her soaking pyjamas. The soot from her hair and face was now running down her front. All Aunt Dorothy had done was make her dirtier than before.

"And don't think you can come inside dripping filthy water everywhere! You will have to dry off before you set foot inside!" ordered Aunt Dorothy. "Now, what was I about to do? I know! Check the barn!"

With that, Aunt Dorothy picked up her shotgun and

marched back over to the barn, a dripping Ruth trailing in her wake.

"Wait! Wait!" cried the girl, but she was ignored.

In no time, they reached the barn door.

"Let me go first!" protested Ruth.

"Get out of my way!" barked Aunt Dorothy, shoving her aside. She stormed into the barn, wielding her shotgun!

BANG! BANG!

CHAPTER 10

A TRAIL OF BLOOD

To Ruth's enormous surprise, the barn was empty. The **alien** was nowhere to be found.

"See?" she said, mightily relieved. "I told you there was no one in here!"

Aunt Dorothy harrumphed. "HUH! I need to call the sheriff right away!"

"Do you really need to call him? He must be very busy!"

"What are you talking about, you great fool! A plane crashed on our farm! Of course I need to call the sheriff!"

"No rush! Tomorrow?"

"No! Not tomorrow! Right now!"

Aunt Dorothy turned, flung her shotgun over her shoulder and strode off across the smouldering field back to her farmhouse.

"Where is our new friend?" Ruth hissed to Yuri.

Immediately, the little dog began following a trail with his nose. It was only when she bent right down and put her face to the ground that Ruth realised her clever little dog had found a trail of blood.

Tiny spots of red dotted the ground.

DOT. DOT. DOT.

Who knew **aliens** had red blood just like humans? At least this one did. It must be from its injured knee.

Yuri followed the trail with increasing excitement.

"SNIFF! SNIFF! SNIFF!"

Despite him having only three legs, Ruth found it hard to keep up with Yuri now. Together, they raced around the **ostrich** pen until the trail stopped. Dead. With nothing more to sniff, Yuri began chasing his own tail.

"WOOF! WOOF! WOOF!" he barked.

Ruth searched the ground for more flecks of blood, but there weren't any.

Not one.

She looked up at the morning sky.

Perhaps the **alien** had been teleported off Earth and shot back up into outer space?

No. Ruth would have seen something while putting out the fires.

There were no trees around to hide behind.

The only structure nearby was the well. Had the **alien** crawled all the way from the barn and hidden inside?

Ruth leaned into the darkness. She heard a noise down there.

SPLOSH!

"Hello?" she called, her words echoing down the shaft. She was sure she heard something moving around in there.

"HELLO?" she called again.

"URGH!" came an echoing sound.

"My wicked aunt and her shotgun have gone now. You are safe. Come on – let me help you out."

But before the **alien** could answer…

WOOH-WOOH! WOOH-WOOH!

It was the wail of a police siren!

The girl stood upright in an instant, banging her head on the hoist.

CLANG!

"OUCH!" exclaimed Ruth, before adding. "WOW! The sheriff is *fast*!"

CHAPTER 11
TOO-TIGHT TROUSERS

RUTH LOOKED ACROSS THE FIELDS. A DUST CLOUD WAS RACING ALONG THE FARM LIKE A TORNADO.

RUMPH!

IT WAS HEADING STRAIGHT TOWARDS HER.

VROOOM!

IN A FLASH, A POLICE CAR BURNED INTO VIEW, THE DUST CLOUD TRAILING BEHIND IT.

THE COWS IN THEIR FIELD SCATTERED.

SCREEEEEEEEE

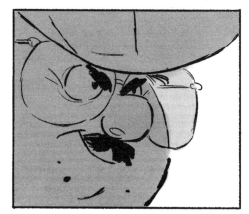

RUTH FELT A PUNCH OF **PANIC.**

IF SHE DIDN'T DO SOMETHING FAST, SHE WAS GOING TO LEAD THE LOCAL SHERIFF RIGHT TO THE **ALIEN!**

EEECH!

Ruth had to look as innocent as possible standing right in front of the well. She crossed her arms. Somehow that felt unnatural, so she uncrossed them and let them dangle by her sides. That felt awkward too. It was as if her arms had only been stuck on a second ago and she had absolutely no clue as to what to do with them.

WOOH-WOOH! WOOH-WOOH!

Ruth settled on hiding her arms behind her back as the police car skidded to a halt.

S C R E E C H !

It stopped an inch from her feet. Yuri retreated behind her legs. The sheriff squeezed his bulk out of his car window. It took quite a while. The man was famous for being fond of doughnuts and, true to form, he had one in his leather-gloved hand. He took a huge bite out of it as if he were a ravenous grizzly bear.

MUNCH!

The bite was so huge that a dollop of strawberry jam squirted out of the doughnut.

SPLURGE!

The dollop of jam landed SLAP-BANG in Ruth's eye.

PLONGE!

The sheriff was a sight to behold...

Cowboy hat

Matchstick
for chewing
permanently
in mouth

Dark glasses

Light dusting of
doughnut sugar

Driving
gloves

Tiny moustache
(far too small
for his face)

Jam stains

Gold
sheriff's badge

Unknown
stains

Handcuffs

Cowboy boots

"Good morning to you, Miss Ruth," began the sheriff, completely ignoring her jammy eye. Sugar sprayed out of his mouth with every syllable.

"Oh! Good morning, Sheriff!" chirped the girl, pretending to be over the moon to see him. "And what a super morning it is too!"

"We don't have time for all that!"

"No?"

"No! I raced right here, sirens blazing, as I just took an emergency call from your aunt, Miss Dorothy," he began in his deep drawl. The sheriff meant business. So there could be no doubt of this, he hoisted up his leg and rested a clumpy foot on the wall of the well.

THONT!

His tight trousers ripped at this movement, right along the bottom.

RIP!

Now you could see his undercrackers!

He put his leg back down again slowly. Then he felt the back of his trousers.

"Not again!" he murmured to himself.

"So Aunt Dorothy called you," said Ruth, her tone far too surprised to be believed. "Whatever about?"

Her arms felt stiff behind her back, so she returned them to her front. They dangled there as if they belonged to someone else entirely.

Perhaps an orang-utan.

"Miss Dorothy told me there was a plane crash right here on the farm last night!" replied the sheriff, bemused.

"Oh yes, there was a plane crash! Silly me! I completely forgot!"

The sheriff's eyes **bulged.** The man knew a lie when he heard one. He put his greasy nose right next to Ruth's and looked deep into her eyes. That way, he would be sure to spot a lie. And this young lady clearly dealt in WHOPPERS!

Keeping his gaze firmly fixed on hers, he spoke very deliberately and slowly.

"You don't have a plane crash here on your farm every night, do you?"

Ruth gulped. How was she going to get out of this one?

CHAPTER 12

WHOPPERS

Ruth pretended to think about the sheriff's question.

"Not EVERY night, no," she began. "We didn't have any plane crashes on the farm at all at the weekend. Or last week. Or last month. Or last year. Or the year before that. Or the year before that one. In fact, come to think of it, it's never, ever happened before!" she concluded, wiping the jam out of her eye, and sucking it off her finger.

"MMM!"

The jam was truly SCRUMPTIOUS!

"URGH!"

It was a moan from down the well!

"What was that?" demanded the sheriff.

"What was what?" replied Ruth, even though she knew exactly what was what.

"That sound!"

"What sound?" she asked.

"It was like a moaning sound!" pressed the sheriff.

"**URGH!**" it echoed once more.

"There it is again!"

"Oh, that?" asked Ruth. "Just my tummy rumbling!" Another one of her **whoppers.** "I haven't had breakfast. **Ever!** Please could I have just one of your spare doughnuts?"

From out of the corner of her eye, she'd spied a big box of them on the passenger seat of the police car.

Jam ones. Custard ones. Chocolate ones. Cream ones. Ring ones. Ones with hundreds and thousands sprinkled on top. They were all crying out to be eaten.

"I am so sorry, Miss Ruth, but I only bought a dozen," replied the sheriff, shaking his head and taking another bite.

CHOMP!

"I understand," she replied, although she didn't.

"So, Miss Ruth, did you see this airplane fall out of the sky?"

"No."

"But your Aunt Dorothy once told me that you have a telescope up in your attic room at the top of the house."

"Yes."

"So you were staring up at the night sky, but you didn't see a thing?"

Ruth shook her head so much that her cheeks wibble-wobbled.

"Is that a 'no'?" he pressed.

"Yes. Er, I mean, yes, that's a no. I didn't see a thing! I was fast asleep." Another **whopper!**

The sheriff leaned in so close that Ruth got a gust of black-coffee breath.

BLEURGH!

It smelled so sour. YUCK! Why did grown-ups drink gallons of the stuff? It was disgusting.

"Asleep? Is that so?" queried the sheriff.

Ruth nodded her head. "Fast asleep. Snoring away! Dreaming of butterflies and unicorns and fairies, like us children do. Then a **BANG** woke me up. I ran out and saw the wreckage of what was definitely one hundred per cent, no doubt about it, cross my heart and hope to die, an airplane!"

The sheriff's sugar-dusted moustache twitched in disbelief. "Were there any survivors?"

Ruth bowed her head sorrowfully. "No."

WHOPPER!

To make it more dramatic, she attempted to force out a tear, but none came. Instead, she pretended to blink one away, sniffing to add some colour to her performance.

"SNIFF!"

"You are completely sure there were no survivors?" he pressed.

"Yes. Well, actually, no."

"No?"

"Yes, and no."

"Yes, and no?"

"No. Yes. No. I don't know."

The sheriff shook his head. This girl's answers were becoming weirder and weirder by the minute. They must all be WHOPPERS! "Has your little dog here sniffed out any survivors?"

"No one at all! Isn't that right, Yuri?" Ruth looked down at him. Like a very good dog, he shook his head. Even he was WHOPPING now.

"Well, I think it's high time I began some detective work of my own," mused the sheriff, stuffing the last hunk of one of the dozen doughnuts into his mouth. "Don't you?"

Ruth shrugged, which made her look GUILTY!

The hefty man began ambling around the crash site. Wherever he spotted a singed patch of ground, he bent down to look for clues, his knees clicking each time.

SNAP! SNAP!

He picked up the charred fragments of metal from the flying saucer one by one and inspected them, evidently feeling like a genius detective.

"There's not much left of this airplane, is there?" he asked.

"No," agreed Ruth. "I think it is unlikely it will ever fly again."

The sheriff raised his caterpillar eyebrows. "You don't say!"

Then, out of the corner of his eye, he spotted something strange.

The pod.

Or, rather, what was left of it.

The sheriff was not an intelligent man; he probably couldn't even spell the word. However, it didn't take a genius to realise that this wide, round glass pod did **not** belong on an aeroplane.

"This don't look like no airplane," remarked the sheriff. He peered inside the charred and smashed bubble. "Well, I'll be darned. I seen one of these at the movies! This must be one of them **FUOs!**"

Ruth broke into a cold sweat.

"Well, I imagine you are a busy man, Sheriff," she babbled. "I don't want to take up any more of your precious time. Thank you so much for stopping by. Do come again soon!"

"One of them **FUOs!** In this old town! Well, I'll be darned!"

The sheriff took off his cowboy hat and hurled it into the air.

He tried to catch it, but failed. No matter, he picked up his now-dusty hat and performed a little celebratory dance!

"Yee-ha!"

He danced all around the well. Ruth looked on nervously and prayed there weren't any more moans from down there.

Fortunately, after just one lap of the well, the sheriff was completely puffed out.

"HUH!" he gasped.

Perhaps fearing that he might collapse, he leaned heavily on Ruth's shoulder. She felt as if she were going to be pushed into the centre of the Earth by his bulk.

"HUH! HUH! HUH!"

"Are you all right?" asked Ruth, a fair bit shorter than she had been a moment ago.

"I think I need some water. Let me grab some from your well," he said, reaching out for the bucket.

Ruth panicked. NO! The **alien** was down there!

CHAPTER 13

IT SPEAKS!

"NO!" said Ruth.

"No what?" asked the sheriff.

"No water!"

"Why?"

"No time! You need to get going!"

"I do?"

"Yes! You have important police business to attend to! Doughnuts to eat. Sirens to wail. Pants to split!"

"I do! We haven't had so much drama in this town since old Farmer Gideon's goat gobbled down his wife's bloomers!" he announced. "An **FUO!** A flying unidentified odour? This is big! This is bigger than big! This is BIGGEROONEY! I gotta get to the nearest telephone. I gotta call the CIA! I gotta call the FBI! I gotta call the mayor! I gotta call the sheriff! Oh no! I am the sheriff! I know! I gotta call the president!"

Ruth and Yuri watched in disbelief as the bulky man took a running jump and dived through the window of his police car.

WOOMPH!

He landed face down in his own box of doughnuts.

SPLURT!

When he righted himself on the driving seat, his face was a riot of sugar, jam, icing, chocolate, custard, cream and hundreds and thousands.

BEFORE

AFTER

"You stay right there, little lady! Don't you touch a thing!" shouted the sheriff, leaning out of his police-car window. He stamped on the accelerator pedal and the car lurched off at terrific speed.

VROOM!

"I won't!" she lied.

Not that the sheriff could possibly have heard her, as the siren was deafening.

WOOH-WOOH! WOOH-WOOH!

The police car looked as if it were going to rattle to pieces as it zoomed back across the fields.

RATTLE! RUTTLE! ROTTLE!

Yuri couldn't watch any more. He shook his head and covered his eyes with a paw.

Once the car had disappeared in another tornado of dust, Ruth paced back over to the well.

"HELLO!" she called down into the darkness. "ARE YOU STILL THERE?"

It was pitch-black, so Ruth leaned in a little further to see.

As her eyes became accustomed to the dark, she saw that the **alien** was clinging on to the rope.

"DON'T BE SCARED, MY FRIEND!" she said. "THE SHERIFF'S GONE NOW. AND MY AUNT AND HER SHOTGUN ARE BACK AT THE FARMHOUSE. NO ONE IS GOING TO HURT YOU. I PROMISE! HERE. GIVE ME YOUR HAND."

Ruth leaned a little further into the well, her toes lifting off the ground. Like a see-saw she toppled forward, but unlike a see-saw she didn't topple back! She just kept toppling in!

"ARGH!" she cried as she tumbled down the

well. She hit the **alien**. HARD.

B O O F !

"OUCH!" it cried.

Ruth carried on tumbling. She closed her eyes. Was this the end? A gloved hand gripped tightly on to her ankle.

The **alien** had saved her life!

"Thank you," she said as she dangled headfirst down the well.

Yuri barked and barked. "WOOF! WOOF! WOOF! WOOF!" The little dog was in a big panic, so big that he jumped up on to the wall of the well. Having only three legs and an egg whisk, he lost his footing and fell down the well too!

"RUFF!" he yelped.

As Yuri plummeted into the darkness, he struck Ruth.

B A S H !

"ARGH!" cried Ruth as she nosedived down the well.

Yuri just managed to bite on to the back of her pyjamas.

CHOMP!

And somehow the **alien** grabbed hold of the dog's tail.

"RUFF!" yelped Yuri again.

Now all three were hanging down the well in a chain, with a little dog in the middle. One false move and they'd all be history.

Ruth pushed her feet to either side of the well, and despite the slimy walls managed to wedge herself in place. Her little dog then perched on her head, his furry bottom within sniffing distance of her nose.

"I've got you, Yuri!" she said. "Let's get out of here! Now!"

Then she felt her wrist being gripped.

"URGH!" exclaimed the **alien** in effort.

Little by little, she was hoisted up through the darkness into the light.

The next thing she knew, all three were lying in a heap beside the well.

"ARGH!" moaned the **alien**, clutching his leg.

"Your knee!" exclaimed Ruth. "Let me see what I can do!"

Ruth scrambled to all fours. At first the **alien** wouldn't remove its gloved hands from its leg, but the girl reassured it.

"It's OK. We're friends, remember?"

Slowly it did.

"That's nasty," remarked Ruth, inspecting the wound.

The **alien's** knee was all oozy. It must have hit it hard on impact with the Earth.

"We need a bandage!" she said. "I know! Yuri, bite on to my sleeve!"

The little dog did as he was told.

CHOMP!

"Now tug-of-war!"

The pair pulled in opposite directions and BINGO!

RIP!

The arm of Ruth's pyjamas was torn off.

"YES!" she exclaimed. "This will make the perfect bandage!"

Within moments, she'd wrapped it round the **alien's** knee and tied it tight.

"Thank you!" it said.

"IT SPEAKS!"

CHAPTER 14

HIDING PLACE

"YES!" boomed the **alien** from under its tall helmet. It had the spookiest voice, like a giant speaking from inside a cave.

"Well, why didn't you say anything earlier?" asked Ruth.

"I couldn't get a word in edgeways."

This made Ruth laugh. She did talk a lot. "Yes. I do tend to babble! I have about a billion questions for you!"

"All in good time!"

"What can I call you?"

"Spaceboy! That is what I call myself."

"Cool name! Hello, Spaceboy! So, you're a boy?"

"YES! How about you?"

"Well, some people think I am a boy because I cut my hair short and am into space, but that's so behind the times. It is the 1960s for goodness' sake!"

"I am into space too!"

"You're from outer space!"

"Oh yes!"

A distant siren wailed.

WOOH! WOOH! WOOH!

"Oh no!" exclaimed Ruth. "Not him again!"

"They *can't* find me!" boomed the **alien**, panic in his voice.

"Why?"

"Because, if they do, I will be in terrible danger!"

"How do you know?"

"I KNOW!"

"Then we need to hide you! Come on, Spaceboy!"

Ruth and Yuri led a limping Spaceboy to a distant corner of the farm. Not far from the pen of **ostriches,** a wonky garage squatted. It was home to Aunt Dorothy's ancient farm vehicles. The tractor and combine harvester were both broken down and rusty, ready for the scrapyard. But it cost money to have them repaired or towed away, so Aunt Dorothy had left them there to rot.

When she was little, Ruth used to clamber up on to the tractor. She'd put Yuri in front and sit there happily for hours turning the wheel and making engine noises.

"BRUM! BRUMM! BRUMMM!"

Ruth had the most marvellous dream of escaping to a far-off land, a world away from her cruel aunt. There she would find her mum and dad again. Of course, it was all in her imagination. Still, it gave Ruth comfort.

Her **DREAM** was the one thing Aunt Dorothy couldn't take away from her.

No one ever went in the garage, and even if they did Ruth knew plenty of good places to hide an **alien**…

Inside the stack of spare tyres

In the combine harvester

Behind the hay bales

Up in the rafters

Behind the toolbox

In the old tin bath

Behind the gas tank

Underneath the worktop

Under the old dust sheet

When the pair forced open the door to the garage, Spaceboy was instantly interested in the tractor.

"That's called a tractor," announced Ruth. "A tractor. Trac-tor. It is what us humans use to work on a farm."

"TRACTOR!" repeated Spaceboy. In moments, he was tinkering with the engine.

"You're wasting your time with that silly old thing. It hasn't worked for years!" said Ruth.

But Spaceboy ignored her. With his gloved hands, he continued meddling with wires, tweaking knobs and turning dials.

Ruth and Yuri shared a look. What was this **otherworldly** figure up to now?

Still, there seemed no point in stopping him. Spaceboy could hardly make the old wreck any worse. He continued fiddling with every little part of the engine – parts of which Ruth didn't even know the names of.

Then the most extraordinary thing happened. Spaceboy turned the key in the ignition and for the first time in decades the tractor shuddered into life.

SPLUTTER! SPLOTTER!

It sounded like a very old man coughing, but soon hummed as if it were brand new.

BRUMM! BRUMM! BRUMM!

Was Spaceboy **magic?**

CHAPTER 15

GIANT EAGLE

"WOW!" exclaimed Ruth over the noise. "How did you do that?"

"I am good with machines. I made my own flying saucer!"

"WOW!" exclaimed Ruth again. "Hey! I've just had a bright idea! Together we can build you a brand-new flying saucer! And, as we are now friends, best friends, BFFs…"

"WHAT?"

"Best friends forever! Maybe, just maybe, you could take me back to your planet with you!"

"Mmm," mused Spaceboy. He didn't sound so sure. "Let's see!"

Ruth was already too excited to take much notice. She climbed aboard the tractor. Perhaps all those DREAMS of escaping could finally come true! She yanked on the gear stick.

CRUNCH!

Of course, she had never driven the thing for real, and the tractor immediately lurched off like a bull at a rodeo.

VRUMMM!

The **alien** and the little dog leaped out of the way as the tractor crashed into the wall of the garage.

BOOF!

It smashed straight through the planks of wood.

KERUNCH!

"HELP!" cried Ruth. She yanked on the gear stick again.

GRIND!

This time she managed to throw the tractor in reverse.

BRUMM!

BOOF!

It crashed through another wall of the garage.

KERUNCH!

With two walls destroyed, what was left of the roof caved in.

CRASH!

Ruth twisted the steering wheel sharply to avoid any

more destruction. But the tractor began spinning backwards in a circle, like a dog chasing its tail.

WHIRR!

"HELP!" she cried again. Spaceboy limped after the runaway beast, and eventually leaped up on to it. He stamped hard on the brake.

DOOMPH!

The thing shuddered to a halt, coughing and spluttering all the way.

SPLUTTER! SPLOTTER!

Eventually, the engine died.

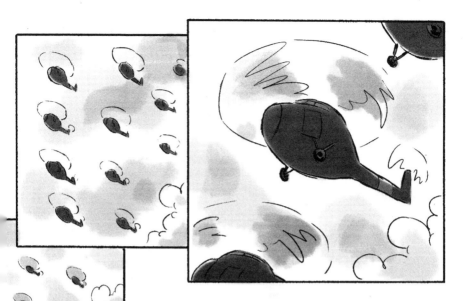

LOOKING UP INTO THE SKY, SHE SPOTTED A FLEET OF HELICOPTERS IN THE DISTANCE. THEY WERE FLYING IN NEAT FORMATION, SPREAD OUT LIKE THE WINGS OF A GIANT EAGLE. WORST OF ALL, THEY WERE HEADING STRAIGHT FOR THEM. TURNING TO HER NEW FRIEND, RUTH SAID:

"YOU ARE RIGHT. IT IS TROUBLE. **BIG TROUBLE!** THEY ARE COMING FOR YOU, SPACEBOY. THEY ARE ALL COMING FOR **YOU!**"

PART TWO

SPACE ODDITY

CHAPTER 16

A DEADLY GAME
OF CHICKEN

A fleet of helicopters flying overhead meant DRAMA. After all, this was a town where nothing exciting ever happened. Here, a missing boot made the front page of the local newspaper.

As the whirring of the helicopter blades grew louder and louder, Ruth shouted over the din: "WE NEED TO HIDE YOU, SPACEBOY! NOW!"

Poor Yuri was shaking, no doubt spooked by the deafening buzz. The little dog leaped up into Ruth's arms. He nuzzled her as her eyes searched the garage for the best hiding place.

In one corner sat some bales of hay. Ruth worked fast to arrange the huge yellow bricks to create a small space underneath where all three could hide.

"PERFECT! OVER HERE!"

She pushed Spaceboy down first by his tall helmet, and then hid herself and Yuri in the gap too.

However, the helicopters must have already been on to them, because they stopped and hovered right over the garage.

The blades were creating nothing short of a hurricane!

WHOOSH!

First, the remaining wooden walls of the garage began to shake.

RATTLE!

Next, the remaining parts of the corrugated iron roof were torn off.

CLUNK!

Then one of the two walls left standing fell outwards.

DOOF!

It was like something from a silent comedy film, except this wasn't funny. It was deadly serious.

Now the bales of hay under which they'd been hiding began flying up into the air.

WHOOSH!

In no time, the three of them were discovered, like ants hiding under a rock. Ruth felt like such a fool. Her clever hiding place had been revealed in a matter of seconds. But she was not giving up the fight yet.

"The tractor!" she shouted over the noise of the spinning blades. Cradling Yuri in her arms, she mounted the tractor, Spaceboy leaping up behind her and holding on tight.

She turned the key in the ignition and...

BRUM!

...the tractor lurched off, crashing through the garage's final wooden wall.

SMASH!

As the three sped off into the field, Ruth looked up over her shoulder. The helicopters were coming down low behind them. They were piloted by sinister hooded figures.

Now the helicopters were hovering on both sides of the tractor! Ruth began to panic. There was no way they could outrun helicopters on this old thing.

"ALLOW ME!" boomed Spaceboy.

He leaned forward and yanked the gear stick.

CRANKLE!

Suddenly, the tractor accelerated.

VROOM!

In seconds, they'd left the helicopters behind.

A smug grin spread across the girl's face. However, that grin soon disappeared when she realised that the sheriff was speeding across the fields in his police car. What's more, there was now someone on the roof with a shotgun!

Aunt Dorothy!

The sheriff must have enlisted her help as a lookout. Now she'd spotted her niece driving a tractor, fleeing from a fleet of helicopters. If there was anything guaranteed to get you grounded, this was it!

The police car swerved to take a path straight at them.

The car and the tractor were locked in a deadly game of chicken.

Who would blink first?

CHAPTER 17

RIDING AN OSTRICH

In a matter of seconds, the police car and the tractor were going to collide.

BANG! BANG!

Aunt Dorothy fired warning shots into the sky.

The noise of the shotgun must have startled the livestock because suddenly the farm's cow and bull scurried into their path.

"MOOO!"

Over the years, Ruth had grown fond of the old cow and even older bull. She would never do anything to put them in danger. So she spun the steering wheel of the tractor.

VROOM!

At the same time, the sheriff sharply changed course in his police car. He and Aunt Dorothy were travelling much faster, and the sudden spin of the wheel caused the car to lean on two wheels and then topple over on to its side. It then **slid** across the field for a few moments before coming to a stop.

KERSHUNT!

Ruth looked back over her shoulder, aghast. Had she caused an accident? Fortunately, Aunt Dorothy and the sheriff were unharmed. The old lady untied herself from the roof and slid down to the ground, while the sheriff squeezed himself out of the car window. Then Aunt Dorothy did something extraordinary. She leaped

on to the back of the cow and began riding it like a horse.

"MOO!"

"GIDDY UP!"

Not wanting to be left out, the sheriff took a running jump on to the back of the bull.

"GROOO!"

"GIDDY UP!"
Unfortunately for him, the sheriff landed looking the wrong way. With the sheriff's bottom facing forward, the bull galloped off. The sheriff did his best to hold on to the animal's hide, but the bull bucked as if it were at a rodeo.

So now Ruth, Spaceboy and Yuri were being pursued by:

A fleet of helicopters... an old lady on a cow... and the sheriff facing the wrong way on a bucking bull.

All this proved a distraction for Ruth. She wasn't looking where she was going. Despite Spaceboy shouting...

"LOOK OUT!"

...and Yuri howling like a wolf...

"HOOO!"

...the tractor hit a stone wall at speed.

KERUNCH!

The force of the impact sent the three flying off the tractor into the air.

WHOOSH!

They landed in the mud in the ostrich pen.

SPLAT! SPLUT! SPLOT!

Not only were Ruth, Yuri and Spaceboy now covered in mud, but their feet (and paws) were also stuck in it.

The helicopters hovered overhead menacingly.

The cow and the bull leaped over the wall and landed in the mud next to the ostrich pen.

SPLAT! SPLUT!

The three were trapped, with the **ostriches** lolloping towards them. Any moment now they could be pecked to death!

PECK! PECK! PECK!

The birds could be brutal.

Just then, Ruth had an idea so bonkers it might just be brilliant. Aunt Dorothy's **ostriches** could finally be put to good use.

"Let's ride these **ostriches!**" suggested Ruth.

"ARE YOU NUTS?" asked Spaceboy.

"YES!" replied the girl proudly.

Ruth knew that although the birds couldn't fly they were surprisingly fast runners. So she took a giant leap of faith as she jumped on to the back of one of the **ostriches.**

THUMP!

"SQUAWK!" squawked the **ostrich,** which was hardly surprising, as it had never had someone riding on its back before.

Immediately, the bird tried to shake the girl off.

"SQUAWK! SQUAWK! SQUAWK!"

But Ruth held on tight and pointed the bird's head forward.

"GIDDY UP!" she ordered.

The bird didn't understand, so she tapped its backside.

TAP!

"SQUAWK!"

Instantly, the **ostrich** sprinted off with Ruth bouncing up and down!

"COME ON!" she shouted back to the others.

Spaceboy was sizing up the **ostriches** hesitantly. However, the sight of Aunt Dorothy on her cow, lowering her shotgun and yelling...

"I GOT YOU, **ALIEN** BOY!"

...made up his mind. He leaped on the back of an **ostrich.**

THUMP!

"SQUAWK!"

From the back of her cow, Aunt Dorothy fired another warning shot into the air.

BANG!

That was all the encouragement Spaceboy's **ostrich** needed. It sped off faster than lightning, the **alien** bouncing up and down on its back.

HURTLE!

That only left Yuri. The three-legged dog shook his head, and then took a running jump. He landed on the back of a baby **ostrich**.

"SQUAWK!"

It too darted off!

Now all three were racing **ostriches** across the pen.
The other **ostriches** scattered to make way.

"SQUAWK!

SQUAWK!

SQUAWK!"

Aunt Dorothy and the sheriff on the cow and the bull were in HOT PURSUIT, having opened the gate and entered the **ostrich** pen.

Then they closed the gate behind them.

Ruth, Yuri and Spaceboy were well and truly **trapped.**

CHAPTER 18

TAKE-OFF

All around the **ostrich** pen stood a tall wire fence.

"There's only one thing for it!" announced Ruth. "We are going to have to make these **ostriches** fly!"

"THESE BIRDS CAN'T FLY!" protested Spaceboy.

"They just haven't learned yet. We have to teach them!"

Yuri shook his head in disbelief.

Aunt Dorothy on her cow and the sheriff on his bull were now dangerously close to our heroes.

Ruth spun her **ostrich** round so she was a good distance from the fence. "Let's do this together!" she said. "We need to make them run as fast as they possibly can! Now, giddy up!"

She tapped her heels on the **ostrich's** sides, and the bird scampered even faster. Spaceboy and Yuri did the same.

"SQUAWK! SQUAWK! SQUAWK!"

The birds were flapping their wings as they attempted take-off. It was either that or they were going to charge SLAP-BANG into a wire fence.

"WAIT FOR IT! WAIT FOR IT!" ordered Ruth.

At the perfect distance from the fence, she shouted, "JUMP!"

The **ostriches** knew what to do. They leaped into the air, flapped their wings and sailed over the fence.

FLAP! FLAP! FLAP!

"**SQUAWK!**

SQUAWK!

SQUAWK!"

Ruth was flabbergasted. They had done it! They were free!

But then, just as Ruth, Spaceboy and Yuri soared into the sky, the helicopters came down super low behind them.

W H I R R !

The hooded figures leaned out of the windows. They were holding **giant** hooks in their hands. One by one, they expertly plucked the three off the backs of the **ostriches** before they had touched the ground.

Ruth was hooked by the back of her pyjamas. "ARGH!"

WHOOSH!

Spaceboy was hooked by the back of his silver spacesuit.

WHOOSH!

"URGH!"

Yuri was hooked by the back of his belt.

WHOOSH!

"GAG!"

"WOOF!"

The three were hoisted high into the air.

"HELP!" cried Ruth.

" N O O O ! " complained Spaceboy.

"RRRUURRRHHH!" howled Yuri.

"ROOOOOOOOOOOOOOOOOOOOO
OOOOOOOOOOOOOOOOOOOOOOOO
OOOOOOOOOOF!" bellowed Aunt Dorothy.

But it was too late. The girl was long gone.

As she dangled in the air, Ruth spotted something strange up ahead. In a field on the next farm loomed three large military-green trucks. Standing alongside them were more figures in radiation suits. These suits were like those that beekeepers wear. Well, if beekeepers were keeping giant radioactive bees.

The figures were dressed in:

Gas masks

Hoods

Shiny all-in-one
white boiler suits

Gloves

Boots

It was clear they weren't taking any chances.

Near the trucks on the ground were three large circles of plastic. They looked like uninflated paddling pools. Before Ruth could wonder what they were, she was lowered on to one, as were Spaceboy and Yuri.

The figures in radiation suits swarmed around the girl, the dog and the **alien**. First, they unhooked them. Second, they jostled them into the dead centre of each circle. Third, they pressed the buttons on three small machines and the circles of plastic began to inflate.

PFT!

PPFFTT!

PPPFFFTTT!

In an instant, the three were imprisoned in giant see-through plastic balls. Then the figures in radiation suits attached cords to the top of the giant plastic balls. The helicopters descended, and the cords were attached to them.

It all happened like clockwork.

A signal was given, then...

WHOOSH!

...the three went swinging through the air.

CHAPTER 19

BALLS

As much as Ruth hated being inside that gigantic clear plastic ball, she hoped someone she knew on the ground might spot her. It is not every day you are dangled from a helicopter in a gigantic clear plastic ball, after all.

To her delight, the helicopters zoomed straight over the dusty old town. She shouted down to the townsfolk, who looked up with their mouths open in wonder.

"HELLO, EVERYONE! IT'S RUTH FROM THE FARM! SO SORRY I CAN'T STOP!"

She was flying! For the first time in her life, she was FLYING! It was the most magical feeling, one she'd waited her whole life to experience. Now it was really happening.

Then the three helicopters soared up to the clouds, flying at an incredible speed. Ruth spotted the huge distance between her feet and the ground, and she didn't like what she saw. GULP!

Ruth thought it best not to look down again. Instead, she turned to her right and saw her mightily confused three-legged dog bouncing up and down in his plastic ball. Yuri was used to chasing balls, not being trapped inside one.

BOING! BOING! BOING!

To her left, she spied Spaceboy in his ball. Despite her
pyjama bandage, his dodgy knee still seemed to be giving
him trouble. It looked as if he was finding it impossible
to keep upright. Soon he was lying on his back like an
upturned beetle.

Undefeated, Spaceboy began swinging the ball from
side to side.

Slowly at first, then it began building up momentum.

As he did so, they passed over deep ravines, the tops of brown brush-covered mountains and lakes as big as oceans.

The ball swung from side to side.

SWOOSH!
SWOOSH!
SWOOSH!

This was **NUTTIER** than **NUTS!** This was **NUTTASTIC!**

Spaceboy's ball bashed into Ruth's…

BOINK!

In turn, hers bashed into Yuri's.

BOINK!

His bashed back into hers…

BOINK!

…which bashed into Spaceboy's.

BOINK!

It was like a game of conkers!

A fatal game of conkers!

One that Ruth needed to STOP!

NOW!

RIGHT NOW!

NOT EVEN RIGHT NOW!

BEFORE THAT!

LIKE BEFORE IT HAD EVEN BEGUN!

What made it so deadly was that the balls were bouncing up dangerously near the blades of the helicopters. Any moment now, one of those balls was going to burst like a balloon.

POP!

Whoever was in it… man, beast or **alien…** was going to end up as tomato ketchup.

SPLAT!

"STOP!" shouted Ruth to Spaceboy, but it was too late.

Spaceboy's bubble bashed into hers.

BOINK!

The force of the impact knocked Ruth clean off her feet.

Gazing up, Ruth could see the helicopter pilots staring down. Judging by their expressions, they appeared to be in a terrible panic. Who could blame them? This was not part of the plan. If this **alien** carried on like this, they were all going to come crashing down to the ground. Helicopters too.

The landscape below was changing rapidly. The patchwork of fields had become a distant memory. Now they were heading out into a vast expanse of desert. It looked like the surface of an **alien** planet. The only part that gave it away as being Planet Earth was a long, straight road, which seemed to lead to the end of the world. Either side of that were giant red rocks, hills and mountains.

Suddenly, the pilots did something that sent Ruth into a spiral of panic, even though they had no choice. They began disconnecting the cables from the bottom of their helicopters.

"NOOOO!" shouted Ruth.

But it was no use.

Within moments the cables were free.

CLUNK!

The three found themselves tumbling through the air in their plastic balls.

"ARGH!" screamed Ruth.

CHAPTER 20

BOUNCE

Time performed the strangest trick. It sped up and slowed down all at once as Ruth, Spaceboy and Yuri the dog plunged for what seemed like miles towards the ground.

Ruth's little life flashed before her eyes...

Arriving at the farm with no shoes on her feet and a sign round her neck

Aunt Dorothy's chilling look

Finding a little three-legged dog on the side of the road and fitting it with an egg whisk

Reading the newspaper story
about the first man in space

Yuri finding the
telescope

Spotting the **UFO**

Finding Spaceboy

Riding an **ostrich**

Being trapped in a
giant plastic ball

That ball falling
through the air at
terrific speed

No! That last bit wasn't a memory. That was really happening. Now! *Right now!*

But there was nothing Ruth could do to stop it. At any moment the ball was going to hit the ground. Hard. She closed her eyes.

Then the most **marvellous** thing happened.

The ball bounced! The ball bounced the biggest bounce that had ever been bounced!

BOING!

It volleyed back up into the air. The exact same thing was happening to Spaceboy and Yuri.

BOING! BOING!

They had bounced on the road, both narrowly avoiding a Greyhound bus, which screeched to a halt.

SCREECH!

Its horn hooted.

BEEP! BEEP!

All three were now hurtling up, up, UP!

But, according to the laws of gravity, what goes up must come down.

BOING! BOING! BOING!

They bounced back on to the road.

BEEP! BEEP!

And again!

BOING! BOING! BOING!

The balls bounced and bounced and bounced. The three inside tried to steer themselves away from the giant rocks dotted on either side of the road, but it was impossible.

It was as if they were in a giant game of pinball!

BOING! BOING! BOING!

Ruth bounced hard.

BOING!

Yuri bounced harder.

BOING!

Spaceboy bounced harder still.

BOING!

Now all three were powering across the desert.

"WOOHOO!" exclaimed Ruth. The girl felt FREE! For the first time in her little life, Ruth believed that nothing and nobody could stop her.

How wrong she was.

Just coming over the horizon was a series of **dark** moving shapes. It was only when the ball slowed a little and Ruth could focus that she realised what they were.

Moon buggies!

They ran on tracks like tanks, with a driver in a radiation suit sitting high up in a pod. The buggies had two long robot arms. One had a grappling hook on the end, like a lucky-dip machine at the fair. The other had a laser blaster!

ZAP!

Who were these figures who kept pursuing them? Ruth was terrified. There was no stopping this hooded army.

Now a dozen moon buggies were heading straight towards them.

The three had to change course.

Ruth looked left.

Moon buggies!

Ruth looked right.

More moon buggies.

Ruth looked behind.

Even more moon buggies!

All were powering over the desert straight towards them.

VROOM!

Clouds of dust and sand were being hurled into the air in their wake.

WHOOMPH!

The moon buggies' tracks made light work of the terrain, crushing small rocks and bulldozing cacti as they sped through the desert to surround Ruth, Yuri and Spaceboy.

The balls eventually stopped short distances from each other.

Ruth felt as if she should take charge. As the other two were an **alien** and an animal, this seemed the most sensible course of action.

"Listen to me!" she said in a loud voice. "There is only one way to escape from these moon buggies…"

Yuri tilted his head as if trying to understand.

"…and that is to bounce OVer them!"

"EXCUSE ME?" boomed Spaceboy.

"Like this!" she exclaimed, and she sprang up and down to make her giant ball bounce.

BOING! BOING!
BOING!

Within moments, the three of them were springing up and down in their balls.

BOING! BOING!
BOING!

"YES!" exclaimed Ruth, trying her best to sound as if she had no doubt whatsoever that her plan would work a treat.

Following her lead, the other two began bouncing their balls straight towards the moon buggies too.

BOING! BOING!
BOING!

Soon Ruth was sure she was bouncing higher than the moon buggies. Now it was all about timing.

BOING! BOING!
BOING!

"WAIT FOR IT!" she shouted, holding her nerve as the moon buggies thundered straight towards them from every angle. There was now a circle of moon buggies closing in on them.

"WAIT FOR IT... WAIT FOR IT... NOW!" cried Ruth.

With that, she bounced down on her plastic ball as hard as she could.

BOING!

Once again, the other two followed her lead.

BOING!
BOING!

ALL THREE BALLS SAILED OVER THE MOON BUGGIES.
THEY LANDED BEHIND THE VEHICLES ON THE DESERT PLAIN.

THE DRIVERS OF THE MOON BUGGIES MUST NOT HAVE SEEN THAT COMING,
AS THEY CRASHED STRAIGHT INTO EACH OTHER.

KERUNCH

WHOOSH!

SUDDENLY THE MOON BUGGIES WERE LIKE INSECTS TRAPPED IN A JAR, TRYING TO CLIMB OVER EACH OTHER WITH ZERO SUCCESS. ALL THEY MANAGED TO DO WAS MANGLE THEMSELVES TOGETHER FURTHER.

AS FOR RUTH, SHE COULDN'T TAKE HER EYES OFF THE CARNAGE SHE HAD CREATED.

Which was a shame, because she wasn't looking where she was rolling.

"WOOF! WOOF!" barked Yuri to warn her, but she was too mesmerised by the mess.

Her ball rolled straight into a cactus.

POP!

And it deflated in an instant.

PLOOF!

CHAPTER 21

POKED IN THE BOTTOM

Ruth felt as deflated as her ball. She tore through the plastic where the cactus had made a hole, and climbed out. The figures in radiation suits began scrambling out of their pods on the moon buggies.

"MAKE A RUN... I MEAN MAKE A ROLL FOR IT!" she shouted to Yuri and Spaceboy.

Neither looked as if they wanted to leave her. Yuri whimpered and did his saddest face. He was an expert at making sad faces, especially when you were eating a sausage and he wanted to save you the bother by wolfing it down for you. What a kind dog.

Spaceboy merely shook his head.

The faceless figures were now little more than an arm's length away. Ruth had to act fast, so she clambered up on to a rock. From there, she jumped on top of Yuri's ball.

BOING!

"RUN, YURI, RUN!"

she shouted down.

The dog instantly knew what to do and began powering the ball through the desert.

TRUNDLE!

Above, like a circus entertainer, Ruth managed to balance and run along the top.

Just as one of the figures was about to grab Spaceboy's ball, Spaceboy rolled off too.

TRUNDLE!

Two of the moon buggies managed to untangle themselves from the wreckage and powered after them. More of the faceless figures leaped on to the sides of the vehicles. They scrambled to their feet, their arms outstretched, ready to catch their prey.

Ruth ran as fast as she could, making Yuri's ball roll faster and faster.

Meanwhile the first moon buggy caught up with Spaceboy's ball. The tip of its laser gun poked it.

POINK!

That just made the ball go faster.

TRUNDLE!

Now Spaceboy's ball overtook Ruth and Yuri's.

WHIZZ!

Being competitive, Ruth ran faster so they caught up again.

ZAP! ZAP! ZAP!

The faceless figures were firing their laser blasters. Explosions were going off all around the plastic balls.

BOOM! BOOM! BOOM!

Not far off, rocks towered like giant tombstones in the earth.

"THIS WAY!" called Ruth. "Maybe we can lose them!"

"If you say so!" replied Spaceboy, unconvinced.

Changing course was harder than she thought, especially with a dog scampering inside the ball below her. It was so hard, in fact, that Ruth lost her footing and slipped.

WHOOPS!

"ARGH!" she cried. She fell forward, but managed to grip on to the ridges of the plastic ball. Now she was lying face down, clinging to the outside of the ball, as it rolled over her every **two seconds.**

"OUCH!"
"OUCH!"
"OUCH!"

Poor Yuri didn't know what to do. Frightened at seeing his mistress's face pressed up against the clear plastic, the little dog sped up, which only made matters worse. Now the ball was rolling over Ruth once **every second.**

"OUCH!"
"OUCH!"
"OUCH!"

The moon buggies with the faceless figures surfing on top were gaining on them. As Ruth rolled round the spinning ball the first moon buggy's laser blaster poked her in the bottom.

"OOF!"

Now she was making exclamations of pain every half a second!

"OUCH!"

"OOF!"

"OUCH!"

"OOF!"

"OUCH!"

"OOF!"

Somehow, Ruth had become a human horn, hooting every time pressure was applied.

It was difficult to know if visitors from other planets have senses of humour. That is until now, because Spaceboy found this bottom-poking absolutely hilarious.

"HA! HA! HA!"

Every time Ruth was poked in the bottom, he let out a **snort** of laughter!

"OUCH!"

"OOF!"

"HA!"

"OUCH!"

"OOF!"

"HA!"

"OUCH!"

"*OOF!*"

"HA!"

Ruth's sour face soured even more.

"THERE IS NOTHING FUNNY OUCH ABOUT BEING POKED IN THE BOTTOM OOF!" she cried.

But this only made Spaceboy snort some more.

"HA! HA! HA!"

Being protective of his mistress, Yuri growled at Spaceboy every time he **snorted.**

"GRRR!"

Together the three were an orchestra of funny noises.

"OUCH!"

"*OOF!*"

"HA!"

"GRRR!"

"OUCH!"

"OOF!"

"HA!"

"GRRR!"

"OUCH!"

"OOF!"

"HA!"

"GRRR!"

However, there was no time to cut a record, as there was some serious escaping to do!

CHAPTER 22

CHOMP!

The plastic balls rolled between a slim gap in the rocks. Slim enough for a large plastic ball to fit through, but fortunately **not** quite wide enough for a moon buggy. The two moon buggies tried to pass through the gap at once. Both ended up smashing straight into the rocks on either side of them.

KERUNCH!

The faceless figures who had leaped on the moon buggies were hurled up into the air by the force of the impact.

They then fell to the ground like rag dolls.

DOOF! DOOF! DOOF!

The moon buggies were now so mangled they couldn't move another inch in any direction.

Our heroes continued rolling down the gap between

the rocks, but as it narrowed the two remaining clear plastic balls became stuck too.

SQUISH! SQUISH!

Poor Ruth was trapped underneath Yuri's ball.

"URGH!" she cried, arching her back to push the thing off. But, try as she might, it just wouldn't budge.

To make matters worse, the faceless figures who'd been thrown off the moon buggies clambered to their feet. In no time, they were hurrying along the gap in the rocks after our three heroes.

"WE'RE STUCK!" shouted Ruth.

"Incredible powers of deduction," remarked Spaceboy, still trapped inside his giant plastic ball.

Suddenly, Ruth had an idea. "I know! Maybe I can bite my way out!" she exclaimed.

"No harm trying!" agreed Spaceboy.

"One big chomp and the ball might just burst!"

CHOMP! CHOMP! CHOMP! she went.

But Ruth's teeth just weren't long or sharp enough to pierce the plastic.

From inside the ball, Yuri placed his face up against hers. The dog tried to lick her face. He did this whenever she was in distress. But it gave Ruth another idea. One much better than her last!

"YOU BITE IT, YURI! YOU BITE IT!" she cried.

Yuri bared his fangs and…

CHOMP!

…the plastic ball exploded like a balloon.

POP!

Ruth scrambled to her feet, cradled her dog in her arms and planted a big kiss on his head.

"Mwah! Good boy, Yuri!"

"ONE DOWN! ONE TO GO!" called out Spaceboy from inside his plastic ball.

The dog knew exactly what to do.

CHOMP!

POP!

Now Spaceboy was free too.

"VERY GOOD BOY, YURI!" he said.

"He's the best! If we go into space, we have to take him!"

"AGREED!" replied Spaceboy.

Ruth couldn't help herself. It had been so long since she'd hugged anyone other than Yuri. She threw open her arms and wrapped them round Spaceboy. He held her tight. For a moment, everything seemed right. It was as if she'd found the piece of her that was missing.

Then, all of a sudden, that part of her *was* missing. One of the faceless figures grabbed Spaceboy by the arm and yanked him back hard.

WHUMP!

"ARGH!" cried Spaceboy.

"GET YOUR HANDS OFF MY FRIEND!" shouted Ruth.

"RUTH! YOU AND YURI RUN AWAY WHILE YOU CAN!" Spaceboy shouted back as he was hauled along the ground.

"I AM NOT LEAVING YOU, SPACEBOY!" she

shouted. "GO GET HIM, YURI!"

The little dog launched himself at the faceless figure.

"GRRR!"

He bit into the arm of the figure's radiation suit and didn't let go.

"GRRR!"

The figure tried to shake the dog off, but it was impossible.

"GRRR!"

This proved to be the perfect distraction.

Ruth grabbed hold of Spaceboy's other arm and yanked him back as hard as she could.

"URGH!"

Spaceboy was FREE!

"LET'S GO, GO, GO, GO, GO!" she shouted.

Holding Spaceboy's hand, with Yuri now at her heels, Ruth raced along the narrow gap in the rocks. She didn't dare look back. That would slow them down. They had to keep moving forward. Away from danger.

Little did they know they were heading straight into it!

CHAPTER 23

BUTT-SLIDING

Up ahead stood a little opening in the rocks. Ruth, Yuri and Spaceboy raced through the hole and very nearly plunged to their deaths!

"HALT!" shouted Ruth as they teetered at the edge of the deepest crater.

It was as deep as a skyscraper is tall.

"WHOA!" exclaimed a wobbly Spaceboy. If his dodgy knee gave way now, it would be the **end**.

Yuri was not so lucky. He was running too fast on his three legs and one egg whisk and careered over the edge! The little dog began sliding down the crater!

"WOOF!" he barked in terror!

Spaceboy grabbed the dog's egg-whisk leg just in time.

YANK!

The **alien** pulled Yuri back to safety.

"Thank you!" said Ruth.

"I have grown rather fond of the little fellow!" said Spaceboy.

"And he has of you!"

Yuri began nuzzling up against Spaceboy's leg to say thank you.

Craters like this were dotted all over the desert. Most

had been caused by meteors hitting Earth thousands or even **millions** of years ago. This one was so vast that it looked as if it had been created by the moon falling out of the sky. It was perfectly round, however, which aroused suspicion. What's more, there was a bare tree trunk standing tall at the very bottom of the crater. This was deep in the desert. There weren't any trees for miles around.

While Ruth was pondering all this, she heard footsteps behind her. Looking over her shoulder, she spotted the faceless figures a few steps away from them. Their arms were outstretched, ready to grab them.

"There's no going back now," said Ruth. "We can only go forward."

"IT'S TOO DANGEROUS!" boomed Spaceboy. "IT IS ME THEY WANT! LET ME GIVE MYSELF UP!"

"NEVER! I know what they will do with you! An **alien** from another world? Experiments and all sorts!" She turned to the two faceless figures behind them. "Am I right?"

The faceless figures nodded.

"But we can't go forward!" remarked Spaceboy. "Look!"

He pointed at a sign to their side that read:

EXTREMELY DANGEROUS DANGER!
KEEP OUT! DON'T EVEN THINK ABOUT IT! REALLY!
GO AWAY NOW BEFORE YOU DIE!

"We have no choice!" said Ruth. "We will have to do some *butt-sliding!* Here goes!"

With that, she took Spaceboy by the hand and Yuri by the paw.

Just as the faceless figures' hands clutched at them, she leaped off the ledge, swinging her companions with her.

"ARGH!" the three cried, as they found themselves sliding into the crater on their bottoms.

WHOOSH!

At first, the walls of the crater were all but vertical.

It was like free falling.

Then they began to slide, as the walls of the crater curved.

"MY SPACEBUTT IS OVERHEATING!" yelled Spaceboy.

Sparks were flying off his silver suit.

SIZZLE! SAZZLE! SUZZLE!

The crater was surprisingly smooth so the three travelled at the speed of lightning.

WHIZZ!

Plumes of red dust shot up into the air behind them.

WHOOMPH!

Ruth looked round to see that their bottoms had rubbed the dust off the crater!

A **silver** surface was revealed underneath in three long butt-sized streaks.

No wonder it felt so smooth, and they were travelling so fast.

This was no ordinary crater!

This was metal!

It was man-made!

Just as Ruth was taking this in, she realised they were heading straight for the tree trunk.

At any moment they were going to –

TWANG!

Too late! They had hit the "tree". HARD! That too was metal.

The force of the blow knocked some of the plastic "bark" off the tree.

KERUMBLE!

As the three found themselves in a dusty heap at the bottom of the crater, Ruth realised where they were.

"THIS IS NO CRATER! LOOK! It must be a giant radar dish!" she exclaimed.

"You are right, Ruth!" agreed Spaceboy.

"WOOF!" added Yuri.

Looking up, they spotted that there were now hundreds of faceless figures lining the rim of the radar dish.

"We are done for!" said Ruth.

"There must be a way to escape!" said Spaceboy.

"I am so sorry! This was a bad idea! We should have stayed and fought!" said Ruth.

"Against this army?"

Just then the three felt the floor sliding underneath them.

A gap was opened and *WHOOSH!*

The three plunged down it.

"ARGH!"

"URGH!"

"WOOF!"

CHAPTER 24

AN INTERGALACTIC CARWASH

It was the world's longest *slide.* The three skidded down it for what seemed like a very long time, their cries echoing along the tube.

"ARGH!"

"URGH!"

"WOOF!"

Just as abruptly as the slide had begun, it ended.

Ruth, Yuri and Spaceboy were deposited on what felt like a **crash mat.**

THWACK!

THWACK!

THWACK!

They found themselves at the bottom of a vast cave. A cave like no other, as this one was humming with technology: computers, TV screens, giant maps of the solar system.

If our heroes thought they had escaped the figures in radiation suits, they couldn't have been more wrong. Down here among the stalagmites and stalactites, there were hundreds more of them, all standing motionless as they faced the three visitors.

There was an **eerie** silence.

Ruth began praying that someone, anyone – man, beast or indeed **alien** – might let one *rip* to break the ice. Sadly, no one did.

Some of the faceless figures at the front pointed laser blasters at the three and guided them towards a conveyor belt.

SHUFFLE!

The belt powered the three of them into a long glass tunnel, wide enough for a train. All along the outside of the tunnel computers chirped…

BLOOP! BLEEP!

…as more figures in radiation suits hurried around

them. They were pressing buttons, twiddling knobs and studying lines on screens. Ruth was trembling with fear. It was as if they were at the centre of some nightmarish **experiment.** She glimpsed X-ray pictures of their skeletons. She heard the beep of heart-monitor machines. She was all but blinded by a piercing red light, which shone straight into her eyes.

What on earth was happening to them?

Next, the three were sprayed with water.

SWOOSH!

The water was freezing cold.

Ruth gasped for breath. "HUH!"

All the dirt and red dust ran down their legs and on to the belt. Then, as they travelled further down the tunnel, little sprays appeared and they were squirted with soap.

SQUELCH!

It wasn't normal soap. It was some strong-smelling chemical.

WHIFF!

It burned a little. If you left it on too long, it seemed as if it might peel your skin off.

SIZZLE!

"GRRR!" growled Yuri.

Spaceboy did everything he could to wipe it off.

Now the conveyor belt took them to a tree of robot arms. All these robot arms had mops attached to the ends.

WHIZZ!

The arms whirred this way and that, washing all the soap off with precision.

Next, there was a blast of hot air from what looked like a giant hairdryer.

BLAST!

All three of them were bone dry in a second. It left Yuri's fur all spiky, and he suddenly looked like a completely different dog.

Next, they passed through a ring of sensors that made a peculiar humming sound.

HUMMM!

A laser scanned their bodies. To her left and right, Ruth spotted the figures in radiation suits studying the screens on their computers with great interest. One nodded to the other and eventually the conveyor belt lurched to a halt.

SHUNT!

"Shall we blast them to oblivion, ***Major?***" asked one of the figures.

Just then three laser blasters on robot arms pointed straight at our heroes.

Ruth scrunched up her eyes as tight as they could go. Was she going to be vaporised?

"Not just yet, Captain," replied a deep-voiced faceless figure.

A very relieved Ruth, Yuri and Spaceboy stepped out of the tunnel. They were all cleaner, drier and more confused than when they'd gone in.

The sea of figures in radiation suits parted to let one particular person through. He had an embroidered name badge sewn on to his radiation suit, which read: **MAJOR MAJORS. HEAD OF THE TOP-SECRET SECRET BASE.** Judging by the speed at which all the others stepped out of his way, it was clear that he was their leader. Every step he took he clinked, clanked and clunked.

Some of the crowd were holding movie cameras to record this historic moment.

"Welcome to Planet Earth," the major said to Spaceboy, reaching out a gloved hand to shake.

The **alien** reached his out, and the two hands touched.

"WE HAVE MADE FIRST CONTACT!" announced the major.

There were huge whoops and cheers from all the others.

"WOOH!"

The major's handshake must have been incredibly strong as Spaceboy wilted like a flower.

Next, **Major Majors** took off his head covering and suit to reveal an army uniform underneath, adorned with what looked like one hundred medals. That was what all the clinking, clanking and clunking was about. As well as being a war hero, the major was pointlessly tall and stupidly handsome. His ageing movie-star face was framed by a short and neat army haircut, which made his head look impressively square. He had piercing blue eyes, a tight mouth that looked as if it never smiled, and a chin so strong you could rest a vase of flowers on it.

"All three have been checked for viruses and radiation," he said. "The **alien**, the girl and the dog. We are all clear. I repeat. ALL CLEAR! SOUND THE BELL!"

At his order, a bell sounded.

DRING!

The others took off their head coverings and radiation suits. A forest of faces adorned the cave, each one more amazed than the last, their wide eyes focused on the **alien**. All were soldiers. If it hadn't already dawned on the three guests, this was a military base.

"Well, you certainly put us all through a wild-goose chase!" continued the major. "The helicopters. The balls. The moon buggies. But you found your way here just perfectly on your own! Welcome!"

"Sorry, Spaceboy!" sighed Ruth. "I led you straight into the lion's den."

He shrugged. "They were going to get me sooner or later."

"THE **ALIEN** CAN TALK!" announced *Major Majors*.

There were more huge whoops and cheers from the others.

"WOOH!"

"Yes, of course I talk!" he huffed. "Where are we?"

"In my **TOP-SECRET SECRET BASE**," replied *Major Majors* proudly. "It's **TOP, TOP SECRET** because it is here we, the US military – the best in the world – monitor the skies for interplanetary spacecraft."

"Well, it's not that top secret, because we found it," said Ruth.

"That crater up there is really a giant radar dish," announced *Major Majors*.

"Yes. I figured that out!" she said, slapping her forehead in exasperation.

"All right, smarty-pants! The radar dish tracked the

flying saucer. We have been waiting for a breakthrough like this for years. We even pinpointed the crash site of the **alien** craft. That's when we sent up the choppers to track you down, Spaceboy!"

"Well, ***Major Majors***," began Spaceboy, "it's been so nice to meet you all down in this **TOP-SECRET SECRET BASE** of yours. Good luck with your **TOP-SECRET SECRET** stuff. Now, if you don't mind, I really should be on my way."

Spaceboy took Ruth's hand and turned to go.

But, behind them, the major called out, "Oh no, no, no, my little Space Oddity. You ain't going nowhere!"

PART THREE

LOVING THE ALIEN

CHAPTER 25

DOGKIND

"GULP!"

Ruth was sure she heard Spaceboy gulp under his helmet. The **alien** was nervous. That made her nervous too.

"Spaceboy! Us meeting for the very first time is not only going to win me another medal," announced *Major Majors,* pointing to his clinking, clanking, clunking chest, "it is going to go down as the greatest moment in the history of mankind!"

There was wild applause from his crack military team.

When it stopped, Ruth piped up, "Don't forget dogkind."

"What did you just say, miss?" demanded the major, his piercing blue eyes swivelling to her.

"Dogkind."

"DOGKIND?" he spluttered.

"Yes! Dogkind!"

"What do you mean by 'dogkind'?"

"Dogs! My dog here found the **alien** first," she replied.

Yuri nodded his head and barked. "WOOF!"

The Major turned to the **alien**. "Is this true, Spaceboy?"

"Yes. It is. The dog leaped up on to my flying saucer. At first I thought I had landed on a dog planet."

This made Ruth laugh. "Ha! Ha!"

"A dog planet?" sneered the major.

"A planet where dogs are in charge."

"Dogs in charge of a planet!" mocked the major. "I have a cat. Marilyn. She is my mother's cat really, but Mother lets Marilyn sleep in my bed at night when I get lonely. Clever little creature, is Marilyn. I could imagine a cat planet, where cats are in charge! But never a dog planet!"

"GRRR!" Yuri growled at the man, bearing his fangs.

Major Majors tried again. "THIS IS THE GREATEST MOMENT IN THE HISTORY OF MANKIND, AND DOGKIND!"

Now Yuri barked his approval. "WOOF!"

The man's expression softened, and he tentatively reached out a hand to stroke Yuri.

"What is your dog's name?" he asked.

"Ask him!" replied Ruth with a grin.

Without thinking, **Major Majors** turned to the dog.

"What's your name, doggy?"

This provoked a roar of laughter from Ruth and Spaceboy.

"HA! HA! HA!"

Major Majors realised he'd been had. His face glowed **puce.**

"His name is Yuri," said Ruth.

"Yuri? That sounds like a Russky name!" barked the major.

Yuri growled.

"If you mean Russian, then yes," said Ruth. "But that term is offensive, even for a dog. He is named after the cosmonaut **Yuri Gagarin.** He is my hero."

A collective gasp echoed around the **TOP-SECRET SECRET BASE.** This was shocking news.

"Russians are the enemies of Americans, not their heroes! It's the law!" **Major Majors** leaned over Ruth menacingly. "Not a Russk— I mean, a Russian yourself, are you?"

"No," she replied calmly.

"Well, then, why did you name your dog after a Russian? It's un-American!"

"Because I love space. That's all. And **Yuri Gagarin** was the first man in space. He just happened to be from Russia. But who cares what country he came from? It could have been a woman."

"A woman?" spluttered the major. "In space?"

"Why ever not?" demanded Ruth.

This question clearly foxed the major.

"Well, I er…" For once, he seemed lost for words.

"Go on!" prompted Ruth, handing him the spade for him to dig himself a hole.

"Well, er, a woman in space just wouldn't work. A woman would attract meteors, a woman would accidentally reverse into a black hole, women are not good at reversing, that is a fact, and er…"

"Yes?" said Ruth, waiting for him to dig himself deeper. Even the major's own men were staring down at the floor in embarrassment.

"And, um, they would eat all the chocolate rations in one go! It is well known that women have ZERO self-control when it comes to chocolate!"

"WHAT A LOAD OF BALONEY!" announced Ruth. "With a capital B! Women can do anything a man can do, and they can do it BETTER!"

There followed an awkward silence, interrupted only by Spaceboy clapping.

CLAP! CLAP! CLAP!

"Have you quite finished?" asked the major.

"No," replied Spaceboy, and he clapped some more.

CLAP! CLAP! CLAP!

Even Yuri put his paws together and clapped.

CLAP! CLAP! CLAP!

Eventually they both stopped.

"Thank you!" huffed the major. "Now, Spaceboy, as we have long planned for an **alien** visitor, we need to whisk you off to our *'Welcome to Planet Earth'* room!"

CHAPTER 26

FRENZY

Major Majors led Spaceboy, Ruth and Yuri to a
waiting monorail train in a corner of the cave. It had
"TOP-SECRET SECRET BASE TRAIN" emblazoned
on the side. The train hummed through the maze of
caves. They passed doors with intriguing signs on them.

ALIEN
AUTOPSY
ROOM

TOILET
(HUMANS ONLY)

TOILET
(ALIENS ONLY)

REACTOR ROOM

RADIATION ROOM

INTERGALACTIC
LIBRARY
(SILENCE, PLEASE)

LASER BLASTER
STOREROOM

DECOMPRESSION CHAMBER

RADAR ROOM

SNACK BAR

CRÈCHE

After travelling for some time, the monorail train lurched to a halt outside a door with a sign on it that read:

THE WELCOME-TO-PLANET-EARTH ROOM

Inside, it was like a brand-new cinema with a big screen.

"YES!" exclaimed Ruth. "Is there any popcorn?"

"NO!" snapped *Major Majors*. "Now, Spaceboy, we are going to show you a short film to introduce you to our planet. It covers a lot of ground and speeds up the welcome process. Please take a seat. I will be back shortly."

The three sat down, Yuri jumping up on to Ruth's lap to get comfortable.

The lights dimmed and the cinema screen flickered into life.

Thunderous classical music played.

"WELCOME TO PLANET EARTH!" boomed a voice. The same words appeared in giant letters on the screen.

Ruth had never, ever been to the cinema, and never watched a television set, so was immediately entranced.

"You are the very first **alien** life form to visit our planet. We are so pleased that you chose to come to this little old place we call home. We humans hope you enjoy your stay and do come and visit Planet Earth again soon. Especially America, which is by far the best country on Earth. Planet Earth is not the biggest planet in the solar system, but, although we haven't visited any of the others yet, we like to think ours is number one. That is because Planet Earth is bursting with this thing we humans call... LIFE! Let us now introduce you to some of the life forms you will encounter on your visit here. This is what we humans look like. This is a man."

A naked cartoon man waved on the screen, much to Ruth's amusement.

"Ha! Ha! Ha!"

It felt childish to laugh, but it is not every day you see a naked cartoon man waving at you.

"And this is a woman."

A naked cartoon woman waved on the screen, much to Spaceboy's amusement.

"Heh! Heh! Heh!" he sniggered under his helmet.

"Mankind is the smartest creature on Earth!"

Now it was Yuri's turn to laugh.

"HUH! HUH! HUH!"

"These are some of the animals that you might meet during your stay on Planet Earth. This is a horse. This is a dog."

Yuri panted with approval.

"This is a cat."

Yuri leaped off Ruth's lap and began barking at the cat on the screen.

"WOOF! WOOF! WOOF!"

"YURI!" cried Ruth, but there was no stopping him. The little dog scampered round to the back of the screen to see where he thought the cat was hiding. Ruth chased after him, trying to grab hold of him, but he was too quick for her. "NO CAT! NO CAT!"

"WOOF! WOOF! WOOF!"

Just as she seized him, Yuri wriggled out of her hands.

"THERE IS NO CAT!"

But Yuri was having none of it.

"WOOF! WOOF! WOOF!"

He began running round and round and round again.

"SPACEBOY! HELP!" yelled Ruth, but Spaceboy didn't move. "NOW!" she ordered.

The girl could be fierce when she wanted to be. Quick smart, the **alien** leaped up out of his seat and dashed round the other side of the screen to try to grab hold of the dog.

But all this talk of a cat had sent Yuri into a FRENZY. He ran back round to the front of the screen, and barked and barked and barked at the cat up there.

"WOOF! WOOF! WOOF!"

Then Yuri took a running jump. As he sprang into the air, his mouth opened wide to chomp at the cat.

"GRRR!"

He hit the screen at speed, bursting through it.

RIP!

Yuri tumbled through the
other side, bashing into Spaceboy,
and hitting the **alien** hard
on the head.

CLONK!

Harder than that.

CCLLOONNKK!!

That's better.

This sent the **alien** toppling backwards.

As he hit the floor – DOOF – his tall helmet slid
off his head. His face was revealed for the very first
time!

Ruth couldn't have
been more shocked
by what she saw...

CHAPTER 27

JUST A BOY

It was the face of a **boy.** Not an **alien** at all. Just an ordinary-looking boy. The boy stood up and covered his face with his gloved hands. But it was too late. His secret was out.

"You're just a boy!" she whispered.

"I know," he said in a surprisingly high voice. "I am so sorry I lied to you!"

Ruth felt hurt. Betrayed. Angry. Confused. Tears blossomed in her eyes.

"I thought we were friends."

"We are."

"No, we are not. I have never had a friend before. And when I finally get one it's all just some kind of cruel trick!"

"I didn't mean to trick you!"

"Well, you did! And I hate you!"

The boy shook his head. "Please don't hate me. I can explain."

"Who *are* you?" demanded Ruth angrily. She hated being taken for a fool.

The boy hesitated. "My real name is Kevin."

"An **alien** called Kevin! As if!"

"I am just a boy. A boy named Kevin. Not an **alien** at all. And I live in the very next town to you."

"You what?" This story was becoming stranger and stranger by the second.

"I wanted to run away from home."

"Why?"

"My grandfather. He hates me."

"You live with your grandfather?"

"Yes." He paused. "My parents are gone."

Ruth stared into his eyes. "Mine too," she said eventually.

The boy took a step closer. "Grandpa just drinks whiskey all day. He takes out all his anger at the world on me!"

"My aunt does that too. Not the whiskey part. She does it sober."

"I saw. And heard," said the boy.

"But that still doesn't explain why you pretended to be an **alien,** for goodness' sake!"

The boy gathered his thoughts.

"I tried to run away from home time and time again. But Grandpa always caught me, and I was punished. Not allowed to leave the trailer for days on end. Not allowed to see friends. Not allowed to utter a word, sometimes for weeks on end."

"Sounds like torture."

"It is. So, I knew I had to think bigger. I had to go somewhere Grandpa could never find me. I chose space!"

"*Space?*"

"Yes."

"You were going to run away to –" Ruth could hardly bring herself to say it because it was all so fantastical – "space?"

"Why not? I had less than nothing to lose."

Ruth was lost for words for a moment. As much as she dreamed of blasting off into space, she could never imagine doing anything so wildly dangerous. "For a million reasons! How on earth were you going to even do that?"

"Build my own spacecraft, of course!" replied Kevin. "Which I did. Only it crashed."

"You really built that thing yourself?" asked Ruth.

"Yep. It took me three years!"

"WOW!" Ruth was seriously impressed.

"I read every comic and watched every movie I could about aliens. Aliens use flying saucers, well, in stories, at least. So I set about building one from scrap metal. My grandpa runs a scrap-metal yard so there was no shortage of bits and pieces I could steal and weld together to make a spaceship. The engine was from an old tractor."

"So that's how you fixed Aunt Dorothy's old tractor in the garage!"

"I like to think I'm good with all that stuff! Not that my grandpa ever appreciated it. The round glass pod came from the cockpit of an old helicopter that crashed while dusting crops."

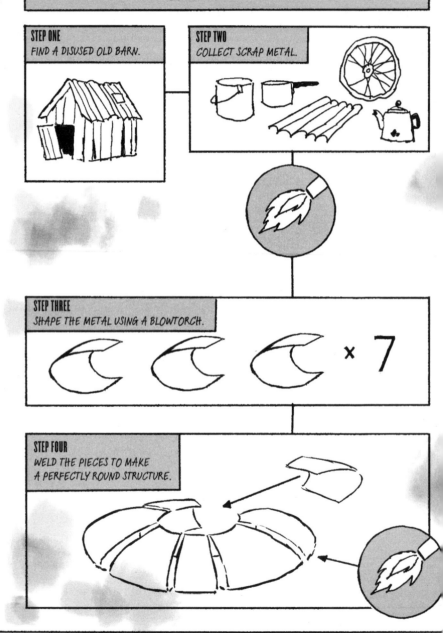

HOW TO BUILD YOUR OWN
FLYING SAUCER*

* DO NOT TRY THIS AT HOME

STEP ONE
FIND A DISUSED OLD BARN.

STEP TWO
COLLECT SCRAP METAL.

STEP THREE
SHAPE THE METAL USING A BLOWTORCH.

× 7

STEP FOUR
WELD THE PIECES TO MAKE
A PERFECTLY ROUND STRUCTURE.

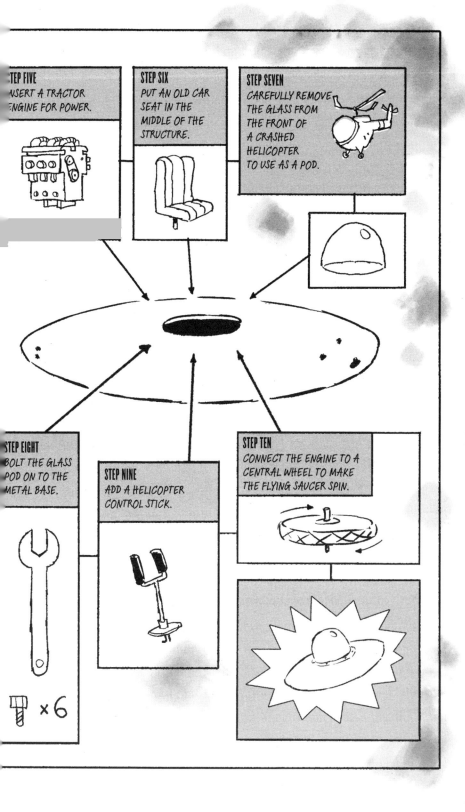

STEP FIVE
INSERT A TRACTOR ENGINE FOR POWER.

STEP SIX
PUT AN OLD CAR SEAT IN THE MIDDLE OF THE STRUCTURE.

STEP SEVEN
CAREFULLY REMOVE THE GLASS FROM THE FRONT OF A CRASHED HELICOPTER TO USE AS A POD.

STEP EIGHT
BOLT THE GLASS POD ON TO THE METAL BASE.

× 6

STEP NINE
ADD A HELICOPTER CONTROL STICK.

STEP TEN
CONNECT THE ENGINE TO A CENTRAL WHEEL TO MAKE THE FLYING SAUCER SPIN.

"But how did you launch that flying saucer of yours into the sky?"

"That was the hard part," replied Kevin. "Some combine harvesters have these wide rubber belts. I tied ten of them together and, using two tree trunks, made a giant catapult."

"That is brilliant! **Bonkers** but brilliant!"

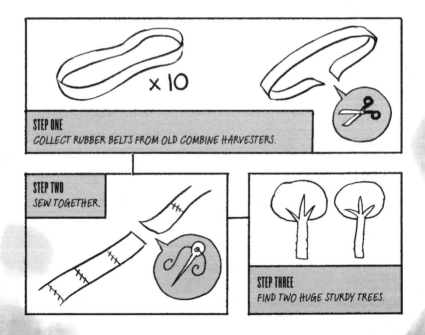

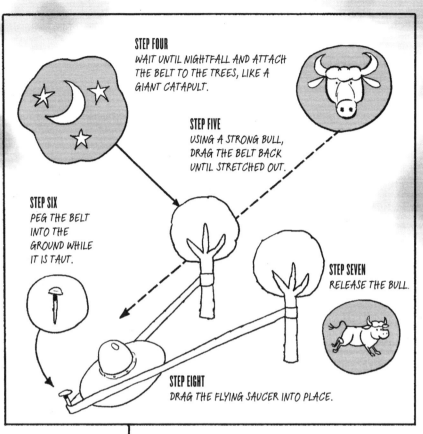

STEP FOUR
WAIT UNTIL NIGHTFALL AND ATTACH THE BELT TO THE TREES, LIKE A GIANT CATAPULT.

STEP FIVE
USING A STRONG BULL, DRAG THE BELT BACK UNTIL STRETCHED OUT.

STEP SIX
PEG THE BELT INTO THE GROUND WHILE IT IS TAUT.

STEP SEVEN
RELEASE THE BULL.

STEP EIGHT
DRAG THE FLYING SAUCER INTO PLACE.

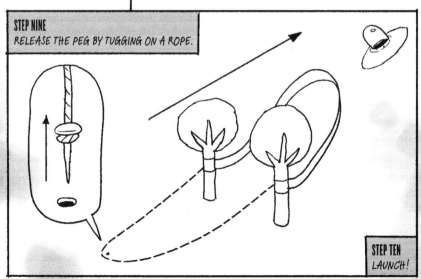

STEP NINE
RELEASE THE PEG BY TUGGING ON A ROPE.

STEP TEN
LAUNCH!

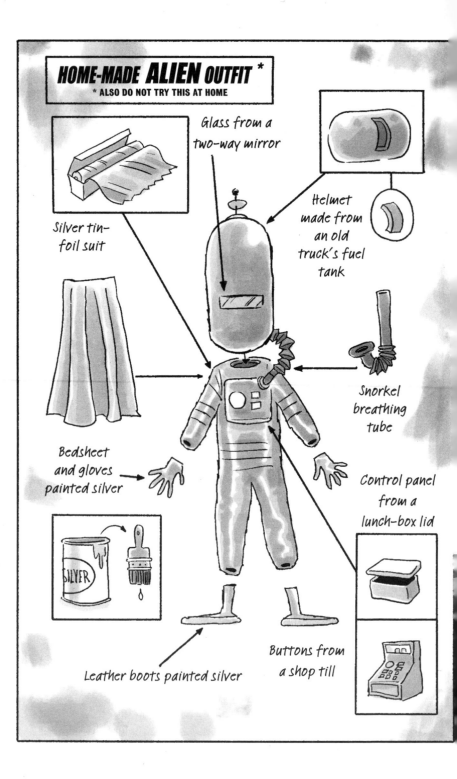

"I made myself a suit from tin foil, and a helmet out of an old truck's fuel tank," continued the boy.

"And so last night I waited until my grandpa was fast asleep," he explained. "He'd been bawling at me for hours and passed out on the sofa in a drunken stupor. I knew I had to seize the moment. I couldn't stand living with him any more! So I took a step into the unknown, and finally launched my flying saucer high into the sky!"

CHAPTER 28

A DEADLY SECRET

"You could have died!" spluttered Ruth.

"I know," replied Kevin. "But I was willing to take that risk."

"That's brave."

"Or stupid."

"You are anything but stupid. You did all this!" she said, indicating his home-made spacesuit. "So what went wrong?"

"There must have been a leak in the fuel tank," he replied, "because as soon as the catapult shot me into the sky and I started the tractor engine, the flying saucer burst into flames!"

As he remembered this, his eyes widened with fear.

"So, the flying saucer fell straight back to Earth?" asked Ruth.

"Yep!" he said sorrowfully. "I nearly hurtled straight

into the farmhouse, but I just managed to skim over the top of it."

"Thank goodness you did."

"Then I crash-landed in the field."

"That's when I found you," said Ruth.

"And I am so glad you did," replied Kevin with a smile. "Otherwise, I might have been blown up in the wreckage."

Ruth smiled back. "But what I don't get is, why keep up the **alien** act?" she said.

"I didn't want anyone to know it was me. If my grandpa found out I have been stealing parts from his scrap-metal yard for years, my life wouldn't be worth living."

"But I wouldn't have told him," replied Ruth.

"I didn't know that, though. I thought it was better if nobody knew. Keep it a deadly secret. But now the lie has run away from me!"

"You can say that again!" agreed Ruth. "What on earth are we going to do now?"

"I don't know. I think I'm going to be in big trouble if these grown-ups ever find out the truth."

"Me too."

"Let's bide our time," he said. "Go along with things. It might even be fun."

Ruth smiled even wider. "I suppose it has been so far. But isn't all this dangerous?"

"I like danger."

"Me too!"

"But we can't keep it up forever. So, when the moment comes, let's all three make a run for it. Disappear somewhere together forever. Far away from all these awful grown-ups."

"Sounds like a great plan!" replied Ruth.

"WOOF!" agreed Yuri.

But just then they heard the door to the **WELCOME-TO-PLANET-EARTH ROOM** swing open.

Kevin was wide-eyed with panic.

"HELP!" he hissed.

Ruth hastily slid the tall helmet back over his head before heaving him to his feet.

Just as he gained his balance, **Major Majors'** face peered through the dog-sized hole in the screen.

"Your dog has damaged government property! You and your mutt need to go back to wherever it is you came from!" he thundered.

"But—" protested Ruth.

"NO!" announced Spaceboy in his spookiest **alien** voice. "THE GIRL AND THE DOG STAY WITH ME OR I WILL BLAST STRAIGHT BACK OFF TO SPACE!"

The major held up one of his huge hands. "Well, not just yet, please, Spaceboy!" he pleaded. "There are some people I would like you to meet. I need to call **the president** right away!" Then he barked an order at one of his underlings. "Fetch me the red telephone!"

CHAPTER 29

THE PINK TELEPHONE

"We can't find the red telephone!" came a shout from far down the cave.

"What do you mean, you can't find the red telephone?" demanded the major.

"We have never, ever used the red telephone before, so no one knows where it is!"

"Well, it must be somewhere!"

"We've looked everywhere!"

"Look again!" ordered the major.

There was a brief silence before the voice replied, "We just have and we still can't find it. We've found the pink telephone!"

Major Majors was spitting feathers. "I can't call the President of the United States on the pink telephone!"

"Why not?" asked Ruth. "He'll never know what colour it is."

"You have a point!" he said. The major then turned and shouted into the darkness. "Bring me the pink telephone at once!"

The pink telephone was handed to the major.

Ruth, Spaceboy and Yuri could only hear the major's side of the conversation, the rest they could only guess.

"Is that the WHITE HOUSE? This is *Major Majors* from THE TOP-SECRET SECRET BASE. Get me the president. This is CODE X. I repeat. CODE X. Ah! Good morning, Mr President. I am calling you on the red, well, reddish

telephone. Oh, I am so sorry to disturb you, Mr President, but this is important news. Very impor—! Of course, I will make it quick, Mr President. I'm sorry, is there a problem on the line? I can hear a loud noise! I'm so sorry, Mr President. I had no idea you were having a presidential pee-pee. No, that's better now. Oh! A bit more? Go right ahead, Mr President. Is that everything? Excellent. Oh dear! Now there is a *really* loud noise! That was you flushing the toilet, Mr President? Of course! You are right – it is always important to flush! No, I don't imagine the First Lady likes it when you don't, Mr President! Let me get right to it. Here at the **TOP-SECRET SECRET BASE** we have made first contact! First contact? With an **alien** life form! No, Mr President, it is definitely not just someone from New York. It is a real-life **alien!** What does it look like?"

Major Majors glanced over at Spaceboy to refresh his memory.

"Not too tall. Wears a lot of silver. Calls himself 'Spaceboy'. Would he like to come over to the WHITE HOUSE? Well, Mr President, I can ask him right now!"

Ruth and Spaceboy shared a worried look. This seemed like a step too far.

"I HAVE OTHER PLANS!" replied Spaceboy.

"He would love to!" lied ***Major Majors***.

"WHAT?" spluttered Ruth.

"We will land on the lawn of the WHITE HOUSE

within the hour, Mr President!"

With that, he clonked the receiver down.

DING!

"Have that pink telephone painted red!" ordered the major. "I can't be using a pink telephone! People will talk!"

"Very good, sir!" came a voice.

"That was the president!" announced **Major Majors**.

"Yep. I guessed that," replied Ruth.

"Prepare the **Megachopper!** We leave at once!" he barked.

Spaceboy's helmet slowly turned to face Ruth.

This whole thing was spiralling way out of control!

CHAPTER 30

DEEPEST DOO-DOO

Within moments, Ruth, Yuri and Spaceboy were back on the monorail. After travelling through miles more of the cave network, they reached a door with a sign on it that read: **MEGACHOPPER**

They were deep below ground in this **TOP-SECRET SECRET BASE.** How on earth could a helicopter take off down here? However, inside this part of the cave, was a gleaming *futuristic* helicopter standing proudly on a helipad. Painted gun-metal grey with blacked-out bulletproof glass windows, it was so heavily armoured that it looked like a flying tank. However, the **Megachopper** did have **TOP-SECRET SECRET BASE AIR** emblazoned in huge letters on the side. That seemed to rather give away that there was a **TOP-SECRET SECRET BASE.** Ruth looked up above the blades of the

Megachopper at the ceiling of rock.

The engine droned into life…

RUMPH!

…as the blades began to spin.

WHIRR!

Ruth, Spaceboy and Yuri were bundled into the back of the helicopter.

Major Majors *is BANANAS!* thought Ruth. *We are all going to die!*

The blades spun faster and faster and faster until she could feel the armoured flying machine lift off the ground. Ruth closed her eyes, and held on tight to Yuri, expecting the worst. In no time, she could feel herself rising higher and higher into the air, so she opened her eyes. To her amazement, the ceiling of rock had slid aside. As the **Megachopper** was now hovering in the open air, the ground below began to close. Just like the radar dish, the whole thing was man-made, but it blended in perfectly with its natural surroundings.

You had to hand it to the people at the **TOP-SECRET SECRET BASE.** They may not have made contact with a real-life **alien** yet, but they had spent some serious wonga on it.

Next, the **Megachopper** spun until its gun-metal grey nose was pointing towards the sun. It paused in the air for a moment before zooming off in the most perfect straight line. It followed that straight line for the entire journey.

The banks of seats in the **Megachopper** faced each other, which felt awkward. On one side sat Ruth, Yuri and Spaceboy. On the other sat *Major Majors* in his military uniform and peaked cap. He had such a carpet of medals that his jacket was barely visible underneath. *Major Majors* had clearly decided he didn't like this uppity little Miss Ruth one bit.

"No more stealing my thunder, miss," he barked.

"I don't know what you mean," protested Ruth.

"I think it best we don't tell the president that it was you who made first contact with the alien."

"Why not?"

"Because, well, because I would like another medal! And, look, I have the perfect space for it just here!" he said, pointing to a space of fabric the size of an ant. "It would make Mother so proud!"

"I am sorry, but you'll have to ask Yuri," she replied. "He met Spaceboy first!"

Major Majors huffed and sulked for the rest of the journey.

Spaceboy stayed well out of it, keeping his head down all the time. He couldn't let his helmet slide off again, or they would all be in DEEPEST **DOO-DOO.**

Here is a handy graph of **doo-doo.**

Not finishing your cabbage

Blowing out all the candles on your brother's or sister's birthday cake

Forgetting to do your homework

Burping at the breakfast table

Falling asleep in class

Peeing in the pool

Scoffing all the cookies in the jar

Being cheeky to the headteacher

Blowing off and blaming it on your grandma

Scrawling a rude word on a wall

Pretending to be an alien from another galaxy

Soon the landscape was changing, as were the colours down there on Earth. The red of the desert rock was replaced by the green of grass and trees. Little Yuri nodded off to sleep.

ZZZZ! ZZZZ! ZZZZ!

Ruth and Spaceboy were offered big bags of potato chips. Spaceboy couldn't risk taking off his helmet, so Ruth ate his bag for him…

MUNCH!

…with a gleeful look in her eyes.

MUNCH!

The pair dozed off for a moment, Spaceboy's head resting on his friend's shoulder, before Ruth's eyes flickered open to see the grey of a big city looming into view. Towers pointed up into the sky like space rockets.

As the unmistakable outline of the WHITE HOUSE – one of the most famous buildings in the world – rolled into view, Spaceboy's dodgy knee began trembling. Ruth put her hand on his and pressed down as hard as she could to reassure him. Instantly the major's suspicion was raised.

"What's the matter with the **alien** now?" he barked over the drone of the **Megachopper** engine.

"Spaceboy's absolutely fine!" lied Ruth.

"I just need a space pee," added Spaceboy.

Ruth had to stop herself from bursting out laughing. She wasn't sure how a space pee was any different from a normal pee, but it sounded funny.

"Do you **aliens** pee in a different way than us humans?" pressed the major.

There was a pause for a moment before Spaceboy replied, **"Alien** pee goes upwards rather than downwards."

"Fascinating!" replied the major, his eyes flickering at the thought. "Maybe there is some military use for pee that goes upwards. Take the enemy by surprise!"

CHAPTER 31

THE MOST POWERFUL MAN ON EARTH

While this conversation about space pee continued, the **Megachopper** set down on the lawn of the WHITE HOUSE. They were moments away from meeting the most powerful man on Earth, the President of the United States of America. Outside the **Megachopper's** tinted window, Ruth could see lines of pristine presidential guards standing to attention. As the door to the chopper swung open, the guards saluted.

There was no doubt that Spaceboy and his two companions were guests of honour.

This only made Ruth's heart pound harder in her chest. Now, just like Spaceboy, she was in deep. It was an uneasy feeling being in on the lie. How long could this boy from the town next door keep up his **alien** act?

As the three were led across the lawn of the WHITE HOUSE by the major, the blades of the **Megachopper** finally shuddered to a stop.

"MR PRESIDENT!" called out *Major Majors* excitedly.

Ruth could hear the distant clunk of a ball being struck.

CLONK!

She looked up to see a small white dot whizzing through the air.

WHOOSH!

She ducked just in time as it skimmed past the top of her head.

WHIZZ!

Major Majors was not so lucky.
The golf ball hit his head…

GONK!

…knocking
him out cold.

THUMP!

He landed on his medals.

CLINK! CLANK! CLUNK!

As **_Major Majors_** lay face down on the lawn of the WHITE HOUSE, nobody was sure what to do.

Fortunately, the familiar figure of the president bounded into view. He was wearing a loud golf outfit, with checks so mismatched that if you looked at him for too long you would get a splitting headache.

"Howdy!" he called across the lawn, holding on to his hair, which on closer inspection looked suspiciously like a toupee. A ginger one at that, even though he had a deep tan. Like his clothes, they did not match. The president was a short, round man, with stubby arms and legs. It would be a miracle if he could reach to wipe his own bottom with those arms.

Behind the president towered a secret serviceman in a dark suit and even darker glasses acting as his caddy, lugging a huge bag of golf clubs.

"You didn't see a golf ball anywhere, did you?" asked the president. "I am something of a champion golfer, but I seem to have lost my ball!"

"It's right here, Mr President!" replied Ruth, picking the hard white ball up off the grass.

"Why thank you," he replied, taking the ball.

He looked down at *Major Majors* lying on the grass. The great military man with all his medals was still out cold.

"What happened to the major?" asked the president.

Ruth looked around at the guards. All were shaking their heads as if to tell her "Don't say a thing".

"Well, I am sorry to say, Mr President, that your

golf ball hit him on the head!"

"I doubt it, young lady. I am a top-class golfer! Number one in the world!"

"Well, then," mused Ruth, "the major's head collided with your ball!"

"That's more like it!" agreed the president. He inspected his golf ball. "Fortunately, my ball was not damaged in any way." He buffed it on his chest and popped it in his pocket.

Next, the president looked at the three guests standing on the lawn of the WHITE HOUSE.

The girl.

The dog.

And the little figure in a silver outfit, cape and helmet.

After a pause, he asked them, "So, which one of you folks is from another galaxy?"

CHAPTER 32

HISTORY IN
THE MAKING

Ruth's mouth opened so wide in shock that she looked like a fish. Perhaps fooling this fool might be easier than she thought! **The president** might be the most powerful man on Earth, but he seemed to be as thick as **ostrich** poop.

"IT IS I!" announced Spaceboy in his spookiest **outer-spaciest** voice. "IT IS I THAT IS THE VISITOR FROM ANOTHER GALAXY!"

"Who said that?" demanded **the president**, more than a little unnerved as he didn't see anyone's lips move.

"He did!" said Ruth, pointing at her friend.

"I! SPACEBOY!" he added, with a little flick of his cape to add some intergalactic drama.

"Ah yes. Of course. I could tell by the voice!" replied **the president**. "Very **alieny.** Follow me!"

The three followed the man into the world-famous WHITE HOUSE, ducking to avoid the end of his golf club, which was bouncing about on his shoulder, and swinging from side to side.

SWOOSH! SWOOSH!

The interior of the WHITE HOUSE was more opulent than anything Ruth had ever seen in her life. It was like a royal palace with deep red carpets, antique furniture and oil paintings adorning the walls. An elegant lady in a floor-length ball gown waltzed round a corner. Her hair had been teased and sprayed into the shape of a bishop's hat. It was taller even than Spaceboy's helmet. "Darling! Get out of those golf clothes and get dressed properly at once! You are going to be late for the banquet!" she barked at the president.

"Sorry, dear. This is the First Lady," said the president by way of introduction.

"THE FIRST LADY WHO EVER LIVED?" asked Spaceboy, much to Ruth's amusement.

"HA! HA!"

"NO!" snapped the First Lady. "I am the First Lady, the wife of the President of the United States of America! Who, may I ask, are you?"

"Oh dear, don't mind him. He's from outer space."

The First Lady looked Spaceboy up and down. "Well, all I can say is I do hope he goes back there! And soon!" She turned to her husband. "Now, put on your dinner suit and for goodness' sake comb your wig – I mean hair!"

"I will, my angel," he replied, smoothing down his ginger toupee. "But first I have to do a live television address to the world!"

"Whatever for?" she asked, wrinkling her nose in contempt.

"This is the first time we have made contact with an alien!"

"So?"

"So, this is a huge moment in history!"

"Well, be quick about it, dear! Or our marriage will be history!"

"Yes, dear!"

She gave one last withering look at the group before waltzing off.

"You're very lucky," began the president. "You caught her in a good mood today."

"I would hate to see her in a bad mood!" quipped Ruth.

"It's not pretty," confided the president. "Oh my! Now, we should be all set up in the Oval Office for the TV address. Wait until the Russians see this! Ha! Ha! First man in space! PAH!"

The Oval Office was the president's official workspace. It sported a rich blue rug and an imposing wooden desk with flags standing proudly behind. There was a large television camera on a stand in the centre of the room, with technical types busying themselves around it. As he entered, they all bowed their heads and mumbled in unison, "Mr President."

"The Oval Office! This is MEGA!" exclaimed Ruth. She set Yuri down on the rug. The little dog rubbed himself all over it, letting out a peculiar moan of pleasure.

"YOW!"

"I must try that," remarked the president in envy. "Now, we are going live to the world in five minutes. Me, talking to a real-life **alien** from that there outer space! This is going to make me look so…"

He searched his mind for the right word.

"Irrelevant?" suggested Ruth cheekily.

"NO!" he snapped angrily. "The opposite of irrelevant! Now, what's the word?"

Ruth was beginning to wonder how this man ever came to be the leader of the free world.

"Relevant?" she suggested.

"That's it! Relevant! Important! And, most crucially, re-electable!"

The girl rolled her eyes and sighed. So this was what it was all about! Grown-ups were all the same! Always out for themselves.

A butler hurried in with a jacket and tie, and dressed the president, as the president checked some notes he'd just been handed. He stared at the page for quite a while with a quizzical look on his face, before

the butler turned it the right way up.

This man really was *DENSE.*

An extra seat was placed beside the desk, and Spaceboy was gestured to sit. Then a technician began

counting down from ten. Ruth and Yuri stood behind a TV monitor, so they could see what the camera was capturing and what the people at home were watching.

Now everyone in the world was going to meet Spaceboy all at once!

"I pray he can fool the world," whispered Ruth to Yuri. "Or we are done for!"

CHAPTER 33

DON'T BE A DORK

"Greetings, folks of Planet Earth," began the president in a slow and serious tone. "This is the President of the United States of America speaking to you live from the HOUSE WHITE."

Ruth and Yuri shook their heads. This man couldn't string a sentence together.

"Today is the most historic day in the history of historic days, and let's be frank, folks, there have been a lot of historic days over our long and historic… history. That is because today the human race, of which I am a member, in case you were wondering – yes, this is my own hair – has made first contact with a creature from another planet. An **alien.** An intelligent life form, well, a reasonably intelligent life form, and he is sitting right next to me now."

Ruth and Yuri watched the monitor as the camera shot widened to reveal Spaceboy sitting next to him.

The president turned to him. "Spaceboy, welcome to my, I mean *our* planet."

He reached out to shake his hand. Spaceboy squeezed too hard, and **the president** winced. "OW! This little **alien** fella's got a firm handshake – I will give him that! And that's history in the making! Well, history has just been made! And truly historic that history was and still is! The very first handshake between a human, that's me, and an **alien,** that's him."

Spaceboy did a naughty thing! He didn't let go of **the president**'s hand.

"Well, I, er…" began **the president**, desperately trying to shake his hand free. Only by wedging his foot on the desk and yanking his hand away did he manage it. "YES!" he exclaimed as he kicked his antique desk, making it topple forward.

WHAM!

It thumped on the carpet, sending everything flying.

WHOOMPH!

It was as if a magician had let a dozen white doves out of a hat at once

as papers flapped in the air.

"Oops!" said the president. "You didn't get that on camera, did you?" he asked.

The cameraman tipped the camera up and down to nod.

"Shucks! Well, who cares about a silly old desk when you have a real-life **alien** in the WHITE HOUSE!"

Ruth and Yuri could barely disguise their laughter at all this, especially when Spaceboy went to shake the president's hand again. He reached out to grab it, but this time the president whipped his hand out of the way, accidentally striking himself on the face in the struggle.

THWACK!

This dislodged the toupee that crouched on top of his head.

The president smiled thinly before turning round and furtively adjusting his toupee. Sadly for him, he managed to spin it round on his head so it was perched back to front. Strands of hair now hung down over his eyes like a pair of curtains. He pulled them apart so he could see once again.

"Ah, there you are!" exclaimed the president. "Spaceboy, I have a few questions for you that I'm sure the people of the world would like to know. First, I have to ask, did you come in peace?"

"No. I came in a flying saucer," Spaceboy replied. His voice was his usual high one, before he corrected himself and made it all **BOOMY** again. "I SAID, 'I CAME IN A FLYING SAUCER!'"

"Yes! I knew that!" huffed the president. "I meant did you come to this planet peacefully?"

"No, it was pretty noisy actually. My flying saucer crash-landed on the ground. Made a great big boom!"

The president coughed nervously. "But you are not going to blow up Planet Earth."

Spaceboy paused long enough for pearls of sweat to pop from the president's forehead.

He finally replied, "I would love to, but I just don't have the time."

"Thank goodness for that!" replied the president, mopping his forehead with his handkerchief. "So, my name is Mr President. We call you Spaceboy, but what is your alien name? What do they call you on your home planet?"

Spaceboy replied not with a word, but with a sound. The sound of a raspberry being blown.

"PFFFFFFFFFFFFFFFFFFFT!"

It was long and low, and for a moment it seemed as if it might never end.

"Your name is…" The president awkwardly pursed his lips and blew a raspberry.

"PFFFFFFFFFFFFFT?"

"NO!" snapped Spaceboy. "PFFFFFFFFF-FFFFFFFFFFFT!"

"Right, and what is the name of the planet you are from?"

"MOONYHINGUNATHENBERG-MONTWITTLEWOOWOOWOO."

This made Ruth snort with laughter so hard she had to grip her nose tight in an effort not to be heard.

"SNORT! SNORT! SNORT!"

The name of the planet was of course impossible to repeat so **the president** didn't even try.

"One of my absolute favourite planets," he lied. "Now, mankind has often pondered the question. It's a big one. We would be honoured if you would answer it for us. Here goes... Is there life on other planets?"

"Yeah! Obviously! Or I wouldn't be here! Duh!" replied Spaceboy. Copying Ruth, he slapped his helmet as if it was his forehead. For a moment it looked as if his helmet might slip off, but he grabbed hold of it just in time.

"PHEW!" murmured Ruth.

"Y-y-yes, of c-c-course," spluttered **the president**, put in his place by this small boy once more. "Have these **alien** life forms heard of me? The most powerful man on Earth?"

"NOPE!"

"None of them?"

"Nope. Not a one. But of course, humans are not the smartest species on Earth."

The president shook his head. "I think you will find we humans are the smarterestest!"

"UH-HUH!" replied Spaceboy, shaking his.

"Well, who on earth is then?" demanded the president.

"Us **aliens** from Planet **Moonyhingunathenberg-montwittlewoowoowoo** have been observing your Planet Earth for centuries before my visit. Our studies have found that the most intelligent beings here are actually... hamsters."

"H A M S T E R S ?" spluttered the president.

"Yep! Hamsters are the most intelligent species by far."

"So, humans are second?"

"Humans don't even make the top ten!"

"WHAT?!"

"It's hamsters, then monkeys, then goats, then bears, then penguins, then hippopotamuses, then ostriches, then worms, then gerbils, then bugs and then humans."

"Right! Well, thank you for sharing that," snapped the president. "Good news for any hamsters watching."

THE MOST INTELLIGENT BEINGS

"Hamsters don't watch TV."

"Why not?" asked the president.

"BECAUSE YOU ARE ALWAYS ON IT!"

There was the sound of chuckling in the Oval Office. Like most jokes, this was serious.

"OK! Smart ass! If they don't watch TV, what do hamsters do all day?"

"Nibble nuts and plan world domination."

"World domination?" spluttered the president.

"When are hamsters going to take over the world?"

"I am very sorry, but that is a secret between me and the hamsters," replied Spaceboy.

"Oh." For a moment the man didn't have a clue what to say. The butler's white-gloved hand thrust a piece of paper under his nose. The panicky president

read it. "Oh! This is a good question I just thought of and definitely haven't just read. Again, it is one that we humans have been searching to find the answer to since the dawn of time. What is the meaning of life?"

A hush descended on the Oval Office. It was so quiet you would have been able to hear an ant fart.

"DON'T BE A **DORK**."

The president turned and addressed the camera.

"So there you have it, folks. The meaning of life is… don't be a **dork!**"

Ruth and Yuri shared a mischievous look. The most powerful man on Earth had fallen for it BIG TIME!

CHAPTER 34

HULLABALOO

There was a flurry of excitement in the Oval Office. The whole world had watched **the president's** live television address. People had crowded around the windows of television shops in the streets just to catch a glimpse of this visitor from another planet. Well, he was really from the town next to Ruth's, but nobody knew that, of course, except her. And Yuri. But neither was about to spill the beans. It was all too much fun fooling the entire world. The question was, how long could they keep up the act?

In moments, every telephone in the WHITE HOUSE began ringing.

RING! RING! RING! RING!

The sound was deafening.

RING! RING! RING! RING!

Yuri howled.

"RURRR!"

Ruth put her hands over Yuri's ears.

RING! RING! RING! RING!

In turn, Spaceboy put his gloved hands over Ruth's ears.

Voices began to call out.

"Mr President, it's Her Majesty the Queen!"

"Mr President, it's His Holiness the Pope!"

"Mr President, it's the Chairman of China!"

"Mr President, it's the Russian Premier!"

"Mr President, it's Elvis!"

The president's face lit up with glee.

"ELVIS! I LOVE ELVIS! What did he want?" he shouted over the hullabaloo!

RING! RING! RING! RING!

"Mr President! They all want to meet Spaceboy!" the voices shouted back.

Ruth beamed. In an instant, Spaceboy had become a SUPERSTAR. More famous than anyone who had ever walked the Earth! Ruth was sure that in no time they could be rich beyond their wildest dreams. In her mind's eye, she saw a whole range of Spaceboy merchandise!

Bowling balls!

Dress-up costumes!

Lunch boxes!

Cuddly toys!

Ice lollies!

Chocolate bars!

Slippers!

Badge sets!

Action figures!

Pencil sets!

Underpants!

Sticker sets!

Soap on a rope!

Helmet egg cups!

School bags!

Jelly moulds!

Board games!

Bubble bath!

Pillowcases!

Even a chewy dog toy for Yuri!

The president began swinging his golf club in time with the telephone rings.

RING! RING! RING! RING!

Holding on to his toupee, he leaped up on to his chair. Then he climbed on to his desk, which had been righted by the butler, and swished his golf club through the air.

SWOOSH!

"Well, tell them all they can't!"

"But, Mr President!" came a chorus of voices.

"Spaceboy is mine! All mine!"

His staff all looked at him as if he had gone BANANAS, even though he had always been BANANAS.

He shouted over the din, "MINE! MINE! MINE!"

Or so he thought.

Because at that moment the doors to the Oval Office burst open and hit the walls.

BANG! BANG!

Suddenly, everybody stopped what they were doing and stood dead still.

The president stopped swinging and started to look more than a little awkward up there on his desk.

In rolled a **chilling** sight.

At first it looked like a robot.

It was a metal box on wheels with what seemed to be arms, four in total. On top of the box was a large glass jar turned upside down.

It was what was in the jar that was most shocking.

At first it looked like a giant egg. In fact, it was a head. A human head. The bald head of an old man. One of the eyes was black with a red light at the centre of it.

A robot eye!

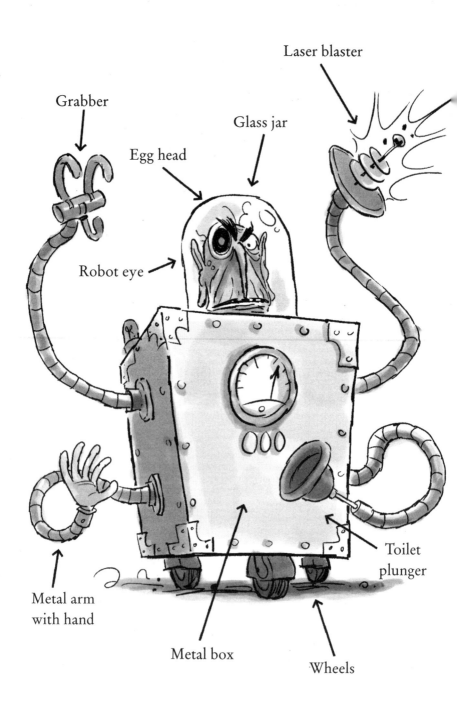

Laser blaster

Grabber

Glass jar

Egg head

Robot eye

Metal arm
with hand

Toilet
plunger

Metal box

Wheels

Ruth wondered if the man were dead. But the other eye blinked and the lips moved. He spoke in a thick German accent.

"No, Mr President! Spaceboy is MINE!"

Ruth, Yuri and Spaceboy all began shaking with nerves.

This man was deeply sinister.

CHAPTER 35

A DARK TURN

"Who are you?" demanded Ruth, suddenly feeling very protective of her new friend, Kevin (also known as Spaceboy).

Yuri leaped down from her arms and began barking at this intruder.

"WOOF! WOOF!"

One of the metal arms on the side of the box pointed in the dog's direction and let out a zap of electricity.

TWOZ!

"YOUCH!" yelped Yuri as he sped off and leaped back up into his mistress's arms. Ruth held her little pet tight.

"Don't hurt my dog!" she exclaimed.

"Next time it barks at me I will put it out of its misery forever!" the head in the jar replied with a **sinister** smile.

The president sheepishly stepped down from his desk. He approached the half man, half robot, sticking out a hand to shake one of the metal appendages, before thinking better of it. He might get zapped too!

"Welcome to the WHITE HOUSE, **Dr Sock!**" said **the president.**

"It's Schock! Not Sock!"

"Well, welcome to the WHITE HOUSE, Doctor!"

"My first and I hope last time," replied the doctor, looking around in disdain at the Oval Office. "That blue rug does not go with those yellow curtains! YUCK!"

"Spaceboy, let me introduce you to the doctor—"

"I will introduce myself!" snapped the head. "I am **Dr Schock.** That's Schock not Sock! S.C.H.O.C.K! Schock! As a young boy, I dreamed only of rockets."

"Me too!" chirped Ruth.

"I was a science genius from the age of two, and soon rose through the ranks of military research. Twenty years ago, the world was at war. I was ordered to create a top-secret rocket bomb by the Führer himself. One that would travel to the edge of space before striking the Earth and **KABOOM!** Happy, carefree, fun-filled days. But late at night one of my rockets exploded by accident. All the scientists at my secret laboratory were killed. Except me. The great indestructible Dr Schock! All they found was my head and my little toe and, as you can see, they put me back together perfectly. And I have to admit I have never felt better!"

With that, Dr Schock made a little twirl on his wheels, knocking over a chair as he did so.

SHUNK!

"The Americans made a deal with me after the war was lost."

"Won, I think?" replied the president.

"Please do not interrupt!"

"Sorry, Dr Sock, I mean Schock!"

"I was told by the American secret service that I would be spared a trial if I came to work with them on their space programme. My rocket dream was still alive! But, right now, the Russians are years ahead of the Americans. They have already put a man in space. Yuri Gagarin."

Yuri the dog nodded his head.

"So the space programme needs your help, Spaceboy. I need you to share all your secrets of **interplanetary** travel with me."

Ruth glowed bright red. She felt as if she were going to burn up. Suddenly, the lie of who was really under that helmet had taken a dark and dangerous turn. This scientific genius was sure to see through him in an instant. Ruth turned to her new friend. She saw beads of sweat trickle down from under his helmet. He was feeling the heat too.

"And if he doesn't want to?" asked Ruth.

"Then I will take Spaceboy to my special laboratory where his **alien** brain can be removed and studied. That way it is sure to spill all its secrets…"

"YES!" chirped Spaceboy in a voice much higher than before. "I WOULD LOVE TO HELP!"

"You see, that wasn't too hard, was it?" purred the doctor. "I am so glad we understand each other. Now, just so I know that I am speaking to a real-life **alien** life form, would you be so kind as to remove your helmet?"

CHAPTER 36

HALF MAN, HALF ROBOT

Was the game up? All eyes turned to Spaceboy. If he took off his helmet, then everyone would know his secret. That he really was just a boy from nowhere. Called Kevin. That was the worst part. Spaceboy was so nervous he let go of the squeakiest bottom blast.

PFFT!

Then he affected the **deepest,** spookiest, **otherworldiest** voice he could. "I CAN NEVER TAKE OFF MY HELMET…" he lied. "AS YOUR EARTH AIR WILL KILL ME."

"That bottom air will kill me," hissed Ruth.

"Shush!" he hissed back.

"Will it, indeed?" thought Dr Schock out loud. "With your permission, Mr President, I will take this thing with me to the **NASA** space centre at *CAPE*

CANAVERAL. We are now tantalisingly close to launching our first American rocket into space."

"All your rockets have crashed, Dr Sock!" replied the president.

"SCHOCK! Thank you for reminding me!" sneered the half man, half robot. "But I am confident that with the secrets we can gather from this intergalactic traveller we will be able to overtake the Russians forever!"

"Good luck!" whispered Ruth.

"Oh no," murmured Spaceboy under his breath.

"What was that?" demanded Dr Schock.

"Nothing!" replied Spaceboy in a high jittery voice, before reverting to his **deep** voice. "NOTHING!"

"Spaceboy! Follow me!" ordered the doctor. His metal box swung round fast. This time his longest protuberance knocked over one of the president's many assistants.

"OOF!"

DOOF!

Spaceboy took Ruth's hand and held on to it tight. They both nodded to the president, who smiled weakly, and began following the doctor out of the Oval Office.

Then Dr Schock came to an abrupt halt. "NO!" he barked. "The girl and her wretched hound have no use in the space centre. They must stay behind."

"N-N-NO!" spluttered Spaceboy. "IF I COME WITH YOU, THEN RUTH AND YURI COME TOO."

That name made the doctor's face contort in fury. "Yuri?"

"Y-y-yes," spluttered Ruth.

"As in **Yuri Gagarin**, the first man in space? The Russian?"

"Yes!"

He spun round, toppling over a bookcase.

KLUNK!

It fell on top of another assistant, who was knocked out instantly.

DONK!

"OOF!"

"I spit on the name **Yuri Gagarin!**" sneered the doctor. With that, he spat hard!

"SPLUT!"

The doctor may have been aiming for the ground, but he must have momentarily forgotten that his head was encased in a glass jar. So, instead, the spit hit the glass.

SPOINK!

Before dribbling down the inside.

DRIBBLE!

He struggled to operate his four protuberances, but none could reach the jar.

"For goodness' sake, someone wipe this sputum off! **THIS INSTANT!**" he shouted, as if it were all their fault.

The assistants all whipped out their handkerchiefs and descended on the glass. But as the spit was on the inside, despite some frantic wiping on the outside…

SQUEAK! SQUEAK! SQUEAK!

…there was absolutely nothing they could do.

"GET AWAY FROM ME, YOU FOOLS!" barked Dr Schock.

They swept as far away from him and his hazardous metal body as fast as they could.

"Then the girl and the dog may come too," he said.

Spaceboy squeezed Ruth's hand tight, and together with Yuri they followed this terrifying half man, half robot out of the Oval Office.

"Have a great day, folks!" called the president after them.

CHAPTER 37

SPACEBOY MANIA

WHIRR!

A **NASA SUPERPLANE** was waiting for them on the lawn of the WHITE HOUSE, ready to whisk our heroes off to the space centre at CAPE CANAVERAL. It was like something from the future, a supersonic aeroplane that had powerful thrusters on its wings so it could take off vertically. There was no need for a runway. The doctor passed ***Major Majors***, who was now sitting up with a bag of ice on his head, then trundled towards the **SUPERPLANE** in his metal box. When he reached it, he activated a mechanism that lifted him up into the air, raising him into the plane.

Meanwhile, a huge crowd had formed all along the outside of the railings of the WHITE HOUSE. People were abandoning their vehicles in the middle of the road and dashing to join them. Soon there was a sea of faces staring in.

Men, women and children were clamouring to catch a glimpse of this visitor from another planet. Mothers were raising their babies aloft so they could witness history in the making. Someone was even holding up their sausage dog, who looked completely uninterested.

There were screams, cheers and shouts when Spaceboy walked across the WHITE HOUSE lawn, his silver cape flapping in the wind.

"WOOH!"

The noise was deafening.

It was nothing short of SPACEBOY MANIA!

The crowd chanted his name, clapped their hands and stamped their feet.

"SPACEBOY! SPACEBOY! SPACEBOY!"

"What shall I do?" he hissed to Ruth.

"I dunno," she hissed back. "Smile and wave! That's what famous people do!"

Spaceboy managed a wave, at least. That was enough for the crowd to go BANANAS.

"HURRAH!"

"I LOVE YOU, SPACEBOY!"

"I LOVE YOU MORE!"

"NO! I LOVE YOU THE MOST!"

Just as Spaceboy, Ruth and Yuri were about to reach the **SUPERPLANE**, a swarm of reporters descended on them. For a moment, Ruth thought they were going to be trampled. They encircled the trio so they couldn't escape, all pointing their cameras and microphones at them. As the cameras clicked and whirred, Ruth did everything she could to hide behind Spaceboy. If she was captured on film, her wicked Aunt Dorothy would know exactly where she was. No doubt, the cruel

old lady would march to the WHITE HOUSE and drag her all the way home by her ear. And it was a very long way.

Shouts from the reporters came thick and fast.

"Spaceboy, are you going to obliterate our planet?"

"Spaceboy, is this the first step in an **alien** invasion?"

"Spaceboy, who made the universe?"

"Spaceboy, did you help build the pyramids in Egypt thousands of years ago?"

"Spaceboy, what exactly is a **'dork'**?"

"Spaceboy, do you eat hamburgers?"

"Spaceboy, do you have a favourite Beatle? John, Paul, George or Ringo?"

"Spaceboy, is this your Earth girlfriend?"

The pack of reporters all fell silent. Someone at the back of the pack went "WOOH!" The others all SHUSHED them as they desperately wanted to hear the answer.

This could be the scoop of the century! A love story across the universe! Just think of the headlines!

The proposal!

The wedding!

The honeymoon!

The children!

Half human and half **alien**!

"NO!" boomed Ruth. "I am not his girlfriend! And I never will be! I don't like boys! Boys make me want to hurl!"

"OOOOOH!" huffed all the reporters.

"NEVER!" agreed Spaceboy. "I DON'T LIKE GIRLS EITHER. THEY MAKE ME WANT TO... SPACEPUKE!"

"BORING!" came a shout.

"GIVE HER A KISS ANYWAY! IT WOULD MAKE A NICE SHOT!" came another.

"NO!" thundered Ruth. "No kisses with boys ever, ever, ever!"

"BOOO!" booed one.

"WELL, SPACEBOY, AT LEAST TAKE OFF YOUR HELMET!"

"YES! GIVE US A GREAT PICTURE!"

"WE JUST WANT TO SEE YOUR **ALIEN** FACE!"

"IS IT, LIKE, ALL WEIRD AND **ALIENY?**"

"NO!" Spaceboy boomed back.

"RUBBISH!"

"COME ON!"

"JUST A PEEK!"

"A LITTLE LOOKSIE!"

"A SNEAKY POOP! I MEAN PEEP!"

Then a forest of hands began reaching out towards Spaceboy's helmet. They wanted to see the face of the very first **alien** to land on Planet Earth. This story was too big to miss.

Yuri growled. "GRRR!"

Ruth tried to slap the hands away. "GET OFF HIM! HE CAN'T BREATHE WITHOUT IT!"

But more and more just kept coming.

"JUST FOR A MOMENT!"

"A BIT OF EARTH AIR CAN'T HARM HIM!"

"WHO CARES IF HE DIES! IT WOULD MAKE A GREAT PICTURE!"

Now there were ten or more hands clasped on to the helmet, with more joining all the time. Spaceboy was using all his might to stop it from being whipped off. If his identity were exposed, the boy would be in **DEEP DOO-DOO.** But it was no use. Spaceboy just wasn't strong enough to win a tug-of-war with a dozen grown-ups. Just as his spotty chin was looming dangerously into view, there was the sound of a **HUGE THUD.**

Most of the reporters were knocked to the ground in an instant.

"OUCH!"

"OOF!"

"ARGH!"

"YOW!"

"PLEASE GET YOUR BIG FAT BEHIND OUT OF MY FACE!" came a shout from a reporter at the bottom of the pile of people.

Now Dr Schock was looming over them. He had rammed into the reporters to save Spaceboy.

"Spaceboy's secrets will remain secret for now!" announced the doctor. "Now make way or I will be forced to use my appendages on you!"

The reporters moved aside to make a path for the three.

Ruth, Yuri and Spaceboy made their way to the *SUPERPLANE*.

Looking down out of the window as they took off, Ruth could see that all around the WHITE HOUSE thousands of people had gathered. Traffic had stopped. People were climbing on top of their cars, just to see him. Ruth nudged Spaceboy so he didn't miss the scenes below. The whole city of Washington, DC had come to a standstill. People were everywhere. Hanging out of windows. Climbing statues. Standing on the roofs of tall buildings. All waving up at the **SUPERPLANE** as it rose steadily into the air.

"This lie is like a balloon. It is getting bigger and bigger and bigger," hissed Ruth.

"And any moment now it is going to burst!" agreed Spaceboy.

Yuri couldn't take any more! He covered his eyes with his paws!

PART FOUR

HEROES

CHAPTER 38

A THRONG OF BOFFINS

In no time, the supersonic **SUPERPLANE** reached the **NASA** space centre at CAPE CANAVERAL. Ruth had been obsessed with outer space and space rockets since she could remember. She had never dared to dream that she would ever come here. Girls like her didn't get to visit places like these. Now she was seeing with her own eyes these towering rockets pointing up at the sky. Poised for adventure. To venture into the unknown. To hurl themselves into the infinite.

For Ruth the space centre felt like her **Neverland**. Her **Oz**. Her *Wonderland.*

The girl had seen glimpses of the centre in Aunt Dorothy's old newspapers, but she could never have imagined the vastness of it. From the sky, it looked as wide as a city, with the rockets as tall as skyscrapers.

The **SUPERPLANE** wound its way around one,

HOW TO SPOT A BOFFIN

Big head in which to store big brain

Wild hair

Unruly nostril and ear hair

Wild look in eyes

Wire-framed spectacles

Bushy beard (optional for ladies)

Row of black biros (slightly chewed)

Cookie crumbs in beard

Grubby fingernails

Slight whiff of turnips

Soup-stained bow tie

White laboratory coat

Odd socks

Sandals

before descending to the ground. Waiting there on the tarmac was a throng of boffins.

The boffins all had serious expressions, as if they had never, ever laughed in their lives. Sadly for them, this seriousness was undermined by having their hair and their long white laboratory coats whooshed around wildly by the **SUPERPLANE'S** superthrusters.

WHOOMPH!

Now beards were covering faces, comb-overs were blown over and skirts were inflated like balloons.

Ruth, Yuri and Spaceboy descended from the **SUPERPLANE** with the doctor. As soon as the platform touched the ground, Dr Schock sped straight towards the throng of boffins waiting for him. They scattered like pigeons.

"THIS WAY!" called out the doctor.

In no time, they were inside a cathedral to space exploration.

"WOW!" said Ruth as she passed through the doors and took in the view.

"A bit bigger than the barn where I built my flying saucer," whispered Spaceboy.

It was a white building, longer than a football pitch

and as tall as ten giraffes. It had white floors, white walls and a white ceiling, all illuminated by the brightest white lights. The only colours were the red, white and blue of the vast American flag that was painted on the wall at the far end of the hall.

Everywhere you looked there was something out of this world:

A recreation of the surface of the moon, complete with astronaut, rocket and space buggy…

A vast water tank with people in spacesuits floating around in it, practising how to move in the weightlessness of space…

A model of the solar system hanging from the
ceiling like a giant mobile, with each planet as
big as a football…

A bank of computers as big as bungalows.
They were whirring and chirping away,
spewing out reams and reams of data…

What looked like a terrifying fairground ride, with people in pods being spun round a central axis at stomach-churning speed, getting used to the G-force on blast-off...

Banks of TV screens displaying dazzling views of outer space taken from satellites...

A glass display of giant meteorites that had struck the Earth...

A freezer with a glass door... Inside was a boffin dressed only in his underpants. His teeth were chattering, he was shivering all over and his body had turned blue. The boffin must be experimenting with the freezing cold of space.

That, or he had popped into the freezer for a packet of frozen peas and somehow got trapped inside...

A brand-new gleaming **SPACE ROCKET** stood tall in the centre of the building, its nose nudging the ceiling. It was the most beautiful thing Ruth had ever seen in her life. It made her feel tiny too, and she didn't mind that one bit. That only served to make her realise how epic a space rocket was. What a huge feat of science it was to design it and what a triumph of engineering it was to build it. It was just a shame it didn't work.

Finally, Ruth and Spaceboy spotted something shocking. Every piece of Spaceboy's flying saucer had been collected from Aunt Dorothy's farm. Although the parts were blackened and broken, a troupe of boffins clutching tools and balancing on stepladders surrounded it. They were painstakingly putting it back together!

This made Spaceboy wobbly on his feet. For a moment, Ruth thought he was going to stumble. She reached out her hand to steady him.

"What's the matter?" she hissed.

"It's my flying saucer!" he whispered back.

"So?"

"So when they put it back together they are sure to figure out I am not from outer space."

"Why?"

"Because it was powered by a tractor engine."

"Oh yes," said Ruth, her tummy churning with nerves. "Oops!"

CHAPTER 39

BOOMED

"What is all this chitter-chattering?" demanded Dr Schock.

Without Ruth and Spaceboy realising, he had trundled up behind them.

"Nothing!" chirped Ruth.

"Well, I do hope Spaceboy will be a little more forthcoming in time," purred the doctor. "My **alien** friend, I need you to share all your space secrets with us!"

"THE SECRETS OF SPACE WILL SOON BE YOURS," lied Spaceboy in his spookiest **alienest** voice.

"Excellent!" replied the doctor before one of his boffins handed him a loudhailer. He raised himself up to his full height.

"THIS IS DOCTOR SCHOCK SPEAKING. BOFFINS! MAY I HAVE YOUR ATTENTION, PLEASE?"

His voice boomed around the hall and, in an instant, all the boffins stopped what they were doing, turned and listened. Even the boffin in his underpants in the freezer stopped shivering.

"LET ME INTRODUCE YOU ALL TO OUR VISITOR WHO HAS COME ALL THE WAY FROM ANOTHER PLANET. HIS NAME IS... SPACEBOY!"

There was enthusiastic applause from the boffins.

"SPACEBOY IS GOING TO HELP US WIN THE SPACE RACE AGAINST RUSSIA!"

There was a huge cheer.

"HURRAH!"

"OUR SECRET INTELLIGENCE DIVISION TELLS US THAT THE RUSSIANS ARE SCHEDULED TO LAUNCH THEIR NEXT ROCKET IN A MATTER OF DAYS. BOFFINS! I AM DETERMINED THAT WE WILL SUCCESSFULLY LAUNCH OUR ROCKET BEFORE THEN!"

"HURRAH!"

"THIS **ALIEN** IS OUR SECRET WEAPON!" he boomed, pointing at Spaceboy with one of his robot fingers.

"HURRAH!"

"WE WILL CONQUER SPACE FOREVER!"

This was a bold statement, but was predictably greeted with a huge cheer.

"HURRAH!"

Then the doctor handed the loudhailer back to his boffin and turned to Spaceboy.

"Now is the time, Spaceboy," he purred. "Now is the time when you must share your secrets of **interplanetary** travel with me!"

CHAPTER 40

BOFFIN CENTRAL

Of course, Ruth knew that Spaceboy had never travelled from one planet to another. His flying saucer had crash-landed on the next farm to his! How much longer could they possibly keep up their **alien** act? The further they went, the worse trouble they would be in if they were found out. It didn't bear thinking about.

Dr Schock ushered Ruth, Yuri (who was in her arms) and Spaceboy into what looked like a square wire cage. Actually, it was an elevator. The doctor's robot arm stretched out, his robot hand opened and his robot finger pressed a button. Next, the elevator clanked all the way up to the top of the **ROCKET** that stood proudly in the centre of the room.

WHIRR!

CLUNK!

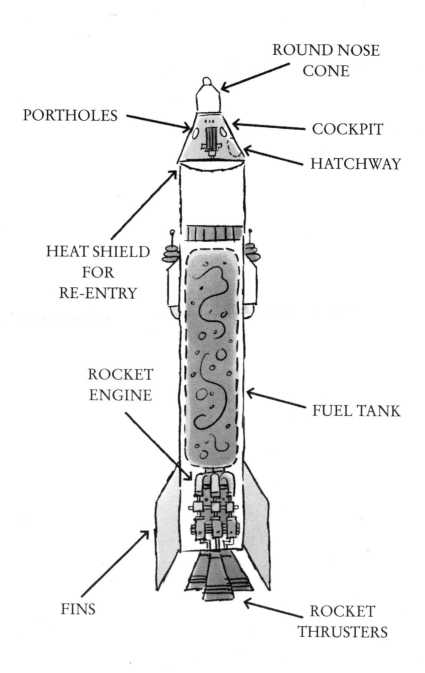

ROUND NOSE
CONE

PORTHOLES

COCKPIT

HATCHWAY

HEAT SHIELD
FOR
RE-ENTRY

ROCKET
ENGINE

FUEL TANK

FINS

ROCKET
THRUSTERS

"I couldn't be prouder. This a boyhood dream come true. Let me present my latest rocket," began Dr Schock. "It was built after the last one crashed on take-off. And the one before that and the one before that and the one before that. And so on and so forth."

"How many of your rockets have crashed?" asked Ruth.

The doctor's lips thinned before he answered. "Twenty-three."

"It was actually twenty-four!" called up a boffin from the base of the rocket.

"ALL RIGHT! ALL RIGHT!" shouted Dr Schock. "TWENTY-FOUR!"

"No. I tell a lie. We had that rocket crash last Tuesday," cried the boffin. "TWENTY-FIVE!"

"Any advances on twenty-five?" called out the doctor, seething.

The boffin checked his clipboard. "No. Twenty-five. But when this one crashes it will be twenty-six!"

"THIS ONE IS NOT GOING TO CRASH!" thundered Dr Schock. "NO MORE COOKIES FOR THAT BOFFIN!" Next, he turned to the **alien.**

"So, Spaceboy, knowing what you know about your

own spacecraft, what would you say might be the flaw in my otherwise genius design?"

Spaceboy peered at the nose of the rocket.

"Well?" demanded the doctor.

"I think I know," piped up Ruth. The girl loved space so much she couldn't resist helping this horror of a man.

The doctor's eyes swivelled towards her. "But you are but a mere female girl! What would you know about space travel?"

"I have studied all the Russian rockets, especially the VOSTOK 1 that blasted Yuri Gagarin into space. And I think I know where you are going wrong."

"Do go on..."

"The nose is too rounded."

"Too rounded?" spluttered Dr Schock.

"Yes!" chimed in Spaceboy, forgetting to do his spooky voice for a moment. Then he remembered. "THE EARTH GIRL IS RIGHT. ALL THE RUSSIAN ROCKETS HAVE POINTY NOSES...!"

"Exactly!" agreed Ruth.

"Remind me to electrocute a selection of my boffins," replied Dr Schock.

"Please don't," said Ruth.

In no time, they were back down on the ground. From there they were brought to an area at the far end of the hall that was swarming with boffins.

Boffins with goggles on using blowtorches… boffins with screwdrivers… boffins drawing plans of rockets… boffins looking at those plans of rockets and stroking their chin beards… boffins 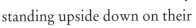 standing upside down on their heads so more blood flowed to their brains… boffins plotting graphs… boffins studying a map of the solar system… boffins blowing their noses… boffins dunking cookies in their tea… boffins removing earwax from their ears with the ends of their Biros and then, when no other boffins were looking, eating it.

This was **BOFFIN CENTRAL**. It was the place where the boffinest of all the boffins put their boffin heads together to solve boffin conundrums that only boffins can solve.*

Dr Schock barked orders at the boffins.

"I have just had a brainwave, boffins! A brainwave so clever it will cause your own pitiful little boffin brains to explode. The head of the rocket should not be rounded, you stupid boffins! It should be pointy!"

Ruth sighed. Another annoying grown-up. Meanwhile, Spaceboy took a blowtorch from one of the boffins. "I need a small length of metal the size of a kitchen utensil to mould into shape."

"I know just the thing!" chirped Ruth, looking down at Yuri's egg-whisk leg.

"WOOF!" barked the dog in protest.

"I can get you another one! I promise!"

"GRRR!" he growled, before rolling over on to his back and letting Ruth unhook the egg whisk.

"Thank you, my little furry ball of love," she said as she tickled his tummy and handed the whisk to Spaceboy.

He immediately set to work.

---

* *If you are partial to sentences with lots of mentions of boffins, this is the book for you. Boffins, boffins, boffins.*

BLAST!

Soon, he had melted the metal and shaped it to make the perfect pointy nose for the rocket.

Now it was ready to be fixed into place.

The question was... **would it work?**

CHAPTER 41

NEW NOSE

Moments later, Ruth, Yuri and Spaceboy were standing with Dr Schock and a boffin back at the top of the platform. All the other boffins on the ground had stopped what they were doing. An otherworldly silence descended on the centre as boffin after boffin gazed upwards to watch Spaceboy solder the new nose on to the rocket.

All that could be heard was the SIZZle of the blowtorch.

SIZZLE! SAZZLE! SUZZLE!

Sparks rained down from the ceiling like fireworks.

FIZZLE! FAZZLE! FUZZLE!

Finally, Ruth inspected his handiwork and nodded.

Yuri barked his approval.

"WOOF!"

"IT IS DONE, DOCTOR SOCK," announced Spaceboy in his spookiest voice.

"SCHOCK!"

"DOCTOR SCHOCK! APOLOGIES! YOUR SPACE ROCKET WILL FLY!"

"Excellent!" said the doctor. "Excellent!" He began clapping with his one robot hand, but all he managed to achieve was to slap his own metal body.

TWUNK! TWUNK! TWUNK!

No matter, the boffins more than made up for him, applauding and cheering as loudly as they could.

"HURRAH!"

"LET'S PREPARE THIS ROCKET FOR TAKE-OFF!" announced Dr Schock.

Just then, there was a huge commotion. The enormous metal doors at the end of the space centre slid open.

KERCHUNK!

A crowd of people rushed in, headed by *Major Majors*.

"STOP!" the military man shouted, still holding a pack of ice to his head.

"WHAT IS THE MEANING OF THIS?" thundered the doctor. He loathed being interrupted.

"DOCTOR SCHOCK!" called out *Major Majors*

from the ground. "Spaceboy isn't who he says he is! This man knows him!"

"Yes!" said an old man, hobbling in on a walking stick. "He's no **alien!** He's my grandson!"

CHAPTER 42

A GINORMOUS RASPBERRY

"GRANDPA!" exclaimed Spaceboy.

Down on the ground, the old man raised his walking stick high into the air and pointed it straight at his grandson.

"KEVIN! You stole the engine out of my tractor to make your stupid flying saucer! Wait until I get my hands on you!"

Grandpa whipped the stick through the air so fast it made a sound.

SWOOSH!

"YES!" piped up one of the boffins who was working on putting the flying saucer back together. "This thing is not from outer space at all. It was powered by a tractor engine!"

Dr Schock's glass jar steamed up in anger.

"TAKE OFF THAT HELMET AT ONCE, SO-CALLED *SPACEBOY*!" he barked. "LET US

SEE YOUR FACE!"

The game was well and truly up. There was nothing more the boy could do. He looked over at Ruth, who nodded. Yuri nodded too. So Spaceboy took off his helmet, and Kevin smiled at the man.

"Oh! Thank goodness for that!" he exclaimed in his usual much higher voice. "It was so hot and stuffy in there! Hello!"

"Don't you *hello* me! Thought you could make a fool out of the great Dr Sock, I mean Schock, did you?"

Ruth pulled a face. "Well, he did, didn't he?"

"SILENCE!" ordered the doctor.

"No, but he did."

"Together we fooled all of you!" added Kevin.

"You didn't fool me, boy!" cried Grandpa. "I recognised that stupid voice of yours from the television when you were speaking to the president!"

"Well, didn't you hear what I said to him?" replied Kevin.

"What do you mean?"

"You didn't listen! I said the meaning of life was don't be a **dork!** And, Grandpa, you are being a **MASSIVE DORK!"**

To no one's surprise, this made Grandpa fly into a rage. "YOU ARE GROUNDED! GROUNDED FOREVER!"

"If I am grounded," began Kevin, "why am I all the way up here? I couldn't be much further off the ground!"

"HA! HA!" chuckled Ruth. She was loving every moment of this.

"Well, boy, you are going to have to answer to the police! I have brought the sheriff!"

"THAT'S ME!" chimed in the sheriff, spraying doughnut crumbs everywhere. "And I hereby arrest this **alien** for

impersonating a human! Or is that the other way around?"

"ROOOOF!" came a cry from the back of the gaggle of grown-ups. The girl would know that voice anywhere. It was, of course, her Aunt Dorothy. "I saw you on the news leaving the WHITE HOUSE. Now come down here this instant, you rotten little maggot!"

327

"NO!" shouted down Ruth.

"ROOOOF! I SAID, 'THIS INSTANT'!" she thundered. "YOU ARE GROUNDED TOO!"

"I SAID NO. N. O. spells NO!" To add emphasis, Ruth did what any child who delighted in being defiant would do. She blew a ginormous raspberry.

"PPPFFFTTT!"

Spittle specks rained down on the grown-ups below.

"YUCK!" complained **Major Majors**. "And Mother just polished my medals!"

"I WILL HAVE MY REVENGE ON ALL THREE OF YOU!" boomed Dr Schock. "Give me that!" he said, wrestling the blowtorch out of Kevin's grasp with one of his robot arms. He twisted the control of the torch, so the flame shot out at full blast.

WHOOOF!

It shot out so far that the flame singed the hairs on Yuri's bottom.

"YOUCH!" yelped the dog, jumping into Ruth's arms.

Then the doctor reversed to get a run-up, or rather roll-up, at the three.

WHIRRR!

As he wasn't looking where he was going, he smashed into the boffin.

BOOF!

He sent the poor man flying off the platform.

"ARGH!" cried the boffin as he fell through the air.

Fortunately, some other boffins caught him.

"Your boffin!" cried Ruth. "He could have been killed!"

"Don't worry. I've got plenty more!" replied the doctor. "Now prepare to die!"

WHIRRR!

Immediately, the half man, half robot sped forward, straight at Ruth, Yuri and Kevin! Any moment now they were going to be shunted off the top of the platform to end up as a splodge on the ground below.

"QUICK!" said Ruth, thinking fast. She grabbed Kevin's hand and together they leaped on to the nose of the rocket, dancing around the new pointy bit.

BOOF!

They landed on their feet, with Ruth still holding Yuri in her arms. The nose was **sizzling** hot from being soldered on, so it was all but impossible to keep standing on it.

"OUCH! OUCH! OUCH!" cried Ruth as her beaten-up leather boots began to fry.

SIZZLE!

All she could do was hop from one foot to the next. Kevin did the same. It looked as if they were doing some fast-paced tap dance.

TAP! TIP! TOP! TUP!

As for Dr Schock, the brakes on his wheels couldn't have been as well-oiled as they should be. They let out a terrific screech as he hit them hard.

SCREEEEEEEEEECH!

But it was too little too late.

The doctor soared over the side of the platform.

WHIZZ!

"BOFFINS! CATCH ME!" he yelled as he tumbled through the air.

WHOOSH!

But the boffins weren't boffins for nothing. Boffins were smart. The boffins all scuttled out of the way as fast as they could. Dr Schock's robot body hit the ground hard.

KERUNCH!

It broke into so many pieces that parts of him flew into every corner of the hangar.

CLUNK! CLONK! CLINK! CLANK!

The doctor's head in the jar was caught by a particularly nimble boffin.

"Thank you, boffin," said Dr Schock. "NOW, MY

BOFFINS! ARM YOURSELVES WITH WHATEVER YOU CAN FIND, GET UP THERE AND DESTROY THEM!"

So the band of boffins began arming themselves with anything they could find. Their weaponry included…

Fire extinguishers

Thermometers

Sharp pencils

Rubber tubing

Forceps

Pestles

Wooden corks

Mortars

Bunsen burners

A microscope

Spoons

Clamps

Pipettes

Spatulas

Teabags

Funnels

Tongs

Rubber gloves

A cat

And even a biscuit!

It was quite an arsenal, although the biscuit got eaten before it could be used as a weapon.

CRUNCH!

"EXCELLENT!" announced the doctor's head in the jar. "INTO THE ELEVATOR AT ONCE! LET'S DESTROY THEM! FOREVER!"

CHAPTER 43

BOFFIN'S BOTTOM

On the doctor's order, all the boffins piled into the elevator, as the other grown-ups fought their way in too. The cage was soon full to bursting. All the grown-ups were squished up together, so nobody knew whose arm or leg was whose. Quite soon, people were mistakenly scratching each other's heads, stroking each other's beards and picking each other's noses.

As Ruth, Yuri and Spaceboy danced on top of the hot nose of the rocket, the elevator stayed firmly down below on the ground.

There was an uncomfortable silence inside it, which was broken by the doctor's head in a jar. "For goodness' sake! We can't stand here all day! Someone press the button!"

"I would be able to if this boffin's bottom wasn't in the way!" came a muffled cry.

"That's not my boffin's bottom! It's your boffin's bottom!" came another, which didn't help matters at all.

However, at last the button was pressed by a boffin's nose...

DOINK!

"OUCH!"

...and the elevator began ascending.

"THERE IS NO ESCAPE," shouted the

doctor as they made their way slowly up to the platform.

"Quick! Into the **SPACE ROCKET!**" said Ruth.

"W-w-what?" spluttered Kevin.

"There's nothing left for us down here on Earth. Do you really want to stay here with your rotten old grandpa? Come on – we've both dreamed of this our whole lives."

"You mean we go up into space in that thing?"

"Yep!"

"But we don't know how to fly it!" said Kevin.

"Only one way to find out!"

"You're nuts!"

"*I'm* nuts?" spluttered Ruth. "You made your own flying saucer and launched it into the sky!"

"I guess I am nuts too!"

"That's why I like you! That's why we're friends."

"We are, aren't we…?" said Kevin.

"Yes!" said Ruth. **"Alien** or not. You are the nuttiest person I have ever met!"

"You are the nutty one!"

"We're both nuts! And nuts is good!"

The elevator door was about to open, spilling out a hundred angry grown-ups.

"It's now or never!" said Ruth.

"Let's do it!"

"RUFF!" agreed Yuri.

So together they shimmied down the side of the cockpit. Then they prised open the hatch to the capsule.

The elevator had now reached the top of the platform.

KERSHUNT!

The squashed faces of **Major Majors**, Aunt Dorothy, Grandpa, the sheriff, assorted boffins and Dr Schock's head being carried in a jar were all staring at them.

The elevator door slid open.

CLANK!

The grown-ups tumbled out on to the platform. They began advancing on Ruth, Yuri and Kevin, the boffins brandishing their assorted weaponry.

As our three heroes disappeared into the capsule, disaster struck! Grandpa just managed to grab hold of his grandson's ankle. He yanked hard.

"HELP!" cried Kevin.

Ruth turned round and grabbed hold of Kevin's wrists.

Now she and the old man were locked in a deadly tug-of-war. Deadly because if they both let go at once then Spaceboy would plummet to the ground and become **Splatboy.**

"DON'T JUST STAND THERE!" ordered Dr Schock.

"HELP THE GRANDPOPS!"

So the boffins, **Major Majors**, Aunt Dorothy and the sheriff formed a human chain behind Grandpa. They began heaving with all their might. Strong though Ruth was, she was no match for the might of twenty grown-ups.

Slowly, Kevin was dragged back on to the platform.

"They've got me!" he cried. "Ruth! Save yourself!"

"I am not going anywhere without you!" she shouted. **"YURI! DO SOMETHING!"**

The little three-legged dog was super smart and knew exactly what to do. He leaped from Ruth's shoulders, ran along the boy's arms, back and legs, and leaped down on to the platform. Then he spun round. His head was now in line with Grandpa's bottom. Yuri opened his jaws wide and… CHOMP!

His sharp teeth bit hard into the old man's behind.

CHOMP!

"YOWEE!" screamed the old man in pain. The shock made him lose his grip on his grandson's ankles. The human chain collapsed, and the grown-ups all fell on top of each other.

"OOF!"

"OUCH!"

"ARGH!"

Ruth hauled Kevin safely back into the cockpit, but that still left Yuri stuck on the platform.

"WOOF!" barked the little dog.

Aunt Dorothy grabbed Yuri by his tail.

"YOW!" he yelped.

The wicked old lady squeezed his tail hard as the dog wriggled and wriggled to get away from her.

"WOOF! WOOF! WOOF!"

"That girl is too soft to go anywhere without her precious pooch!" announced Aunt Dorothy.

She was right.

Ruth was torn. She couldn't bear to stay down on Earth with these awful adults a moment longer, but leaving her precious Yuri with them was unthinkable.

"Come on, cry-baby!" Aunt Dorothy called out.

Ruth was sticking her head out of the cockpit door, looking for help.

"What are you going to do now?" demanded Aunt Dorothy.

Ruth loathed this person with a passion. Her aunt had done everything she possibly could to make her life a misery. Ruth was determined not to let her win. Not now. Not ever.

So, without a thought for her own safety, Ruth took a giant leap from the **SPACE ROCKET** back on to the platform.

CLUNK!

"Give me back my dog!" she said.

"NEVER!" replied Aunt Dorothy.

Yuri wriggled and growled.

"GRRRR!"

The boffins surrounded the girl, all brandishing their weapons.

This was a stand-off!

"SPACEBOY!" called Ruth.

"Well, it's Kevin, but yes?" he replied, popping his head out of the cockpit.

"PREPARE FOR *BLAST-OFF!*"

"But that would kill you all!" he protested.

"I SAID *PREPARE FOR BLAST-OFF!* AND THAT'S AN ORDER!"

CHAPTER 44

BLAST-OFF!

Kevin looked shocked, but ducked down into the cockpit.

Soon the rocket began making a deep droning noise.

DDDDDRRRRR!

Instantly, a robot voice could be heard over a loudspeaker.

"ALL SPACE ROCKET SYSTEMS ARE OPERATIONAL!" it announced. "BLAST-OFF WILL BE IN ONE MINUTE AND COUNTING!"

Immediately, the boffins began running around in circles.

"WE NEED TO GET OUT OF HERE!"

"AND FAST!"

"FASTER THAN THAT!"

"THIS WHOLE PLACE WILL BE AN INFERNO!"

"TO THE ELEVATOR!"

They all bundled in, taking **Major Majors**, Aunt Dorothy, the sheriff and Grandpa with them. As Aunt Dorothy was bustled backwards, Ruth plucked Yuri from her grasp and held the dog tight to her chest.

"You can never ground us now!" said Ruth.

"You will die going up in that thing!"

"I don't care. This has always been my DREAM! To blast off into space and leave you far behind. And my DREAMS are mine and mine alone! You can't take them away from me! Goodbye forever, you nasty old crocodile!"

"HISS!" snarled the old reptile.

"WELL, FOR GOODNESS' SAKE, SOMEONE PRESS THE BUTTON!" came a cry from the elevator.

A boffin's bottom backed up on to the control panel and the elevator whirred into life.

"BLAST-OFF WILL BE IN FORTY-FIVE SECONDS AND COUNTING!" boomed the robot voice around the space centre.

The elevator was now descending, and impatient cries could be heard from inside.

"CAN'T THIS THING GO ANY FASTER?"

"KEEP PRESSING THE BUTTON!"

"DID A BOFFIN BLOW OFF?"

"YES. SORRY. IT WAS ME. JUST NERVES."

"IT BLEW RIGHT UP MY NOSE, YOU BRUTE OF A BOFFIN!"

Ruth held her beloved dog in her arms and turned to go.

"BLAST-OFF WILL BE IN THIRTY SECONDS AND COUNTING!"

Just as she was about to leap back over to the space rocket, a voice stopped her.

"Good luck!" it said.

Ruth turned round. It was Dr Schock's head. The jar must have been dropped by the boffin in all the rumpus. The glass had shattered, and the head had rolled out. Now it was lying there like a hooked fish, taking its final breaths.

"What?" she asked.

"Good luck!" he replied.

"Why, thank you," said Ruth, rather shocked at the evil genius's now tender tone.

"As a boy, I DREAMED of going into space in a rocket I had built myself. But that dream will die with me before the day is out. It belongs to you now. Treasure it."

"I will. I promise."

"Don't forget to press the **RED BUTTON** when you reach space. That will jettison the fuel tank. Otherwise, the rocket will break up and you will all die!"

"Thank you," replied Ruth, not sure whether to believe him or not.

"It will be beautiful up there in space. A beauty

that is never-ending."

"Just like the universe itself."

"Exactly. What an adventure you will have!"

"BLAST-OFF WILL BE IN FIFTEEN SECONDS AND COUNTING!"

Down below, the elevator doors opened and all the grown-ups fled the Space Centre faster than rockets.

"RUTH! COME ON!" called out her friend from the cockpit.

"Goodbye, Dr Sock, I mean Schock!" she said.

"Farewell, Fräulein Ruth!"

"BLAST-OFF WILL BE IN TEN SECONDS AND COUNTING!"

Holding Yuri tight in her arms, Ruth took a running jump.

WHOOSH!

"NINE!"

Together they soared off the platform and landed on the top of the rocket.

CLUNK! "EIGHT!"

She didn't land right and immediately felt unsteady on her feet.

"SEVEN!"

The doctor shouted, "SPACEBOY! HELP HER!"

"SIX!"

In an instant, Kevin's head popped out of the cockpit.

"FIVE!"

Just as Ruth and Yuri tumbled forward...

"ARGH!"

"WOOF!"

...he grabbed hold of her hand.

"FOUR!"

With all his might, he dragged them up...

"THREE!"

…and into the cockpit.

"TWO!"

Before shutting the capsule hatch just in time.

"ONE! BLAST-OFF!"

CHAPTER 45

THE RED BUTTON

The cockpit was a cramped, conical space with what looked like a thousand buttons, dials and displays.

"STRAP YOURSELF IN!" shouted Kevin over the roar of the rocket. "THE G-FORCES ARE GOING TO BE NUTS!"

Indeed, they were. The pressure of taking off at this speed made all three of our heroes' faces turn into **jelly.**

BEFORE

AFTER

He and Ruth just managed to secure their seatbelts in time.

CLUNK! CLUNK!

The rocket crashed through the ceiling of the space centre. **KERUNCH!**

The flames from the rocket burned up everything below.

WHOOMPH!

This is what it must feel like to be a bullet shot out of a gun, thought Ruth.

Looking out of the small round portals on the side of the craft, Ruth waved goodbye to her Aunt Dorothy.

"GROUNDED, AM I?" the girl shouted.

Not that Aunt Dorothy could possibly hear over the roar of the rocket. However, she was still looking up in anger, waving a fist. The old crocodile couldn't hurt her any more. No one down on Earth could. For the first time in her life, Ruth felt weightless. Weightless because nobody was weighing her down, and weightless because the rocket had blasted through the Earth's atmosphere and was now hurtling into outer space.

The rocket began shaking wildly.

RATTLE!

IT FELT AS IF THE WHOLE THING WAS GOING TO CRACK INTO A MILLION PIECES.

"THE R-R-RED B-B-BUTTON!"

"W-W-WHAT?"

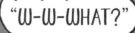

"Dr Schock SAID WE NEED TO PRESS THE **RED BUTTON** TO JETTISON THE FUEL TANKS. OTHERWISE, WE ARE GOING TO D-D-DIE!"

"IT COULD BE A T-T-TRAP!"
"I THOUGHT THAT T-T-TOO!" REPLIED RUTH, FEAR FLICKERING ACROSS HER FACE.

"Maybe that **RED BUTTON** will make the rocket self-destruct."

"You think?"

"Rockets always have a self-destruct button. Press that and it could blow this thing to smithereens!"

"But it feels like we are going to be blown to smithereens if we don't press it!"

"I WISH I KNEW!" shouted Kevin over the noise. "The only spacecraft I ever piloted was a home-made flying saucer."

"Which crashed instantly."

"Now isn't the time, Ruth!"

"Let's push the **RED BUTTON** together!" suggested Ruth. "Then if the spacecraft blows up nobody will get the blame."

"Sound logic!" replied Kevin with a grin.

RATTLE! RATTLE! RATTLE!

"ONE! TWO! THREE! GO!" cried Ruth.

But with their short children's arms it was impossible for either of them to reach the button.

"NO!" cried Ruth, struggling with her harness.

"HOW DO WE GET OUT OF THESE THINGS?" asked Kevin, grappling with his.

RATTLE! RATTLE! RATTLE!

As Ruth continued to wrestle with the straps and buckles, she let go of Yuri.

He floated through the cockpit, paddling the air with his three little legs.

Suddenly, Ruth had a bright idea. The dog could do it! "YURI! PRESS THE **RED BUTTON!**"

RATTLE! RATTLE! RATTLE!

Yuri pushed himself off the top of the capsule so that he was floating straight towards the **RED BUTTON**. He nudged it with his nose.

DONK!

CHAPTER 46

INTO THE INFINITE

There was the longest pause.

Then a lurch as they felt something being jettisoned. A look out of the porthole confirmed that the giant fuel tanks were now floating off into space.

The rattling stopped in an instant. For the first time in a long time, everything seemed calm. Safe. Quiet. Like nothing and nobody could hurt them.

"So, Schock was telling the truth!" said Kevin.

"Yes," she replied. "I guess he wanted the wonder of space to belong to someone. Even if it was us!"

"LOOK AT THE EARTH!" he cried.

Ruth followed Kevin's gaze. Now she too saw a gorgeous globe of blue and green floating in space, surprisingly small.

"Wow," she said, her mouth falling open in wonder. "It's more *beautiful* than I could ever have imagined."

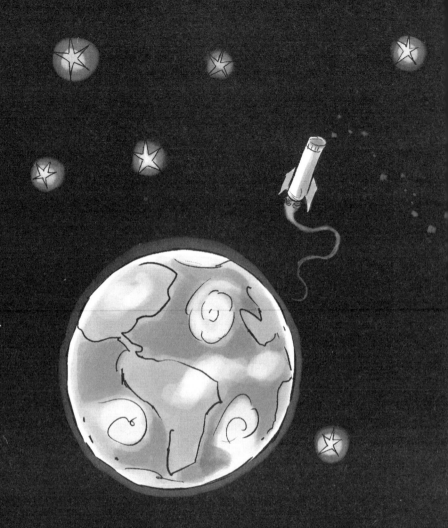

"It really is. Isn't it crazy that the grown-ups in charge down there are always fighting and arguing with each other?"

"Yep," agreed Ruth. "The Earth looks so peaceful from up here."

"If those **dorks** could see how perfect it is, do you think they would want to destroy it with wars?"

"Never! Never in a billion years. You were right all along…"

"DON'T BE A **DORK!**" they said in unison.

"WOOF!" agreed Yuri as he doggy-paddled through the air.

"Where to?" asked Kevin.

"Let's do a quick lap around the universe, Spaceboy."

The boy smiled. He liked that name. "Sounds perfect to me... Spacegirl!"

The girl blushed. She loved being called Spacegirl!

Spaceboy pulled on the steering column as Spacegirl pushed a pedal for power. Spacedog whacked a flashing blue button with his wagging tail, and...

BLAST!

Our three heroes *zoomed* off together into the **infinite**.

THE END

THE SPACE RACE

Spaceboy is a fictional story created by David Walliams, but the space race really did happen. Here is a timeline of ten key moments in the space race between the Soviet Union and the United States of America. The space race began in the mid-1950s and lasted until the collapse of the Soviet Union in 1993.

October 1957

SOVIET UNION. The first artificial Earth satellite, Sputnik 1, is launched into orbit.

November 1957

SOVIET UNION. A dog called Laika becomes the first animal to orbit the Earth, paving the way for human spaceflight. There is now a small monument in Laika's honour in Moscow.

January 1958

USA. Vanguard 1, the first solar electric Earth satellite is launched into orbit. Today, it is the oldest satellite still up in space.

August 1959

USA. The first photograph of Earth from orbit is taken by the Explorer 6 satellite.

September 1959

SOVIET UNION. Luna 2 is the first spacecraft to reach the surface of the moon. And a month later, in October, Luna 3 causes huge excitement by taking the first photographs of the never-before-seen far side of the moon.

January 1961

USA. Ham the chimpanzee is the first great ape launched into space as part of Project Mercury on a flight lasting sixteen minutes and thirty seconds. After his mission to space, Ham lives for seventeen years in the National Zoo in Washington, DC.

April 1961

SOVIET UNION. Yuri Gagarin – Ruth's hero and the inspiration for the name of her pet dog – becomes the first human to journey into outer space. On his return to Earth, Gagarin finds fame as a national hero and celebrity.

May 1961

USA. Just three weeks after the Soviets, Alan Shepard pilots the first US human spaceflight aboard *Freedom 7*. The mission launches from Cape Canaveral – where Ruth and Spaceboy launched their own space adventure.

June 1963

SOVIET UNION. Cosmonaut Valentina Tereshkova is the first woman to go into space. She orbits the Earth forty-eight times and remains today the only woman to have been on a solo space mission.

July 1969

USA. *Apollo 11* lands the first humans on the moon – Commander Neil Armstrong and lunar module pilot Buzz Aldrin. The first step on the lunar surface is broadcast on worldwide live TV, in "one small step for [a] man, one giant leap for mankind".